Jason and

Best wishes,

BLEAK ENCOUNTER AT THE CAPE

A CORNISH ADVENTURE BY SEA AND BY LAKE

RICHARD TRAHAIR

The Book Guild Ltd

First published in Great Britain in 2021 by
The Book Guild Ltd
9 Priory Business Park
Wistow Road, Kibworth
Leicestershire, LE8 0RX
Freephone: 0800 999 2982
www.bookguild.co.uk
Email: info@bookguild.co.uk
Twitter: @bookguild

Typeset in 10pt Garamond Premier Pro

Printed and bound in the UK by TJ Books LTD, Padstow, Cornwall

ISBN 978 1913551 834

British Library Cataloguing in Publication Data.
A catalogue record for this book is available from the British Library.

This book is dedicated to the volunteer watchkeepers of the National Coastwatch Institution who so nobly assist in the protection and preservation of life at sea and along the coastline of England and Wales.

AUTHOR'S NOTE

HAULING MYSELF UP THAT STEEP FLIGHT OF GRANITE steps in the teeth of a north-westerly gale always makes me think of my forebears on that very place, that rocky promontory jutting out westwards into the Atlantic, the only cape in England. Except that it is not really England at all. Englishness, even today, has scarcely penetrated the culture, the 'Mother Earth' spirituality, the mythology of the indigenous people there.

Today visitors might call it vaguely bohemian. The young mums around town wear their hair up and their baggy patchwork trousers faded over ancient lace-up boots. The very air breathes artistic expression in painting, pottery and poetry. The community is classless and mildly radical. The Church struggles to supplant Mother Earth with the Johnny-come-lately doctrine of Christ. (The Nonconformist chapels used to have a greater success rate.) The older generation of West Penwithians are conservative, but not Conservative. They remember the grind of the mines; some of them the graunch of a bouldered seabed overhead as they drilled and sweated for copper, tin and arsenic a mile out under the ocean at Levant.

Further back, in the middle years of the 19th century, my forebears will have struggled against the decline of an agricultural era with sack-laden backs and stoicism; tramping this cape and the adjoining inland fields of Nanpean to feed their meagre sheep and cattle; harvesting the thin crops of hay that crouched against the granite ledges out of the salt-laden horizontal wind forever whipping off the sea, and encouraging their sons to abandon that losing game and turn their eyes eastwards up into England for new lives, hopes and fortunes. In this last endeavour, if not in the others, the outcome was successful beyond their dreams. The spirit of enterprise and the staunchness of faith became the ingredients for my great-grandfather and namesake Richard, and notably his brother William, and their combined offspring together to discard their own grandfather's rearing of foodstuffs for survival on a rocky outcrop of Cornwall, and become suppliers and manufacturers of food products that became familiar the world over, for two-thirds of the 20th century.

But they were Cornishmen. None of them could let go of their roots. All generations, without exception, retained a toehold in the vicinity of Nanpean, and not just for their holidays. A few of the Edwardian and interwar houses in the adjacent town were built and bought by locals with private mortgages provided on otherwise unattainable terms by one or other of my family.

As an inheritor of these loyalties, and a participant all of my life, I walk these fields and coast paths with an adhesive sense of rootedness, although I have never lived here as my permanent home. For the past forty years, home has been five hours' drive away, back up country, back up 't'England'. I write this prologue, then, as the setting for the story which follows. I hope it will help to explain how the extraordinary events recorded therein are so inextricably bound up with the emotional baggage of the author and observer.

CHAPTER
ONE

H E HAD LEFT THE CAR AS USUAL IN THE NATIONAL Trust car park up behind Priest's Cove. Or, more correctly, Just's Cove: Por'Eust – 'Porth Just' in early English. St Just was a shadowy figure, like many Cornish saints; reputed to have murdered his brother, which seems an odd qualification for sanctity. Maybe his brother was irredeemably frightful. These things are relative, I guess. Perhaps a descendant of his had a hand in the dark deeds which I am to relate.

Petroc Tomlyn trudged down from the car park and along the gravel, past the old counting house and other former mine buildings now converted into smart cottages. The sea was up in a big way, the towering swell racing silently in from the horizon, gaping cave-like as it reached the brake of the shallows, each wave curling along its ridge, teetering, and then collapsing forwards in a roar and a rush, its white spume tearing backwards and its black-and-white mass boiling onwards towards the grey rocks fringing the base of the

Cape, its final impact an explosive crack as of a bomb. Then the brilliant white disintegration skywards, and a second collapse into a million fragments of spume anointing each rock like spilt milk, the sea level sucked down and out again in a drum roll of dragging boulders and pebbles, ready to load its successor wave and repeat the sequence again and again for hours or days.

Petroc could feel the vibration of each wave through the ground beneath his boots, its wet, salty residue stinging his face in the onshore gale as he bent his frame around the turn of the path and up the steps towards the little plateau on which stood, miraculously, the insubstantial timber Coastwatch lookout station bravely facing the onslaught from the west.

The flagpole was straining against its stays, the flag stretched eastwards as though it were starched, as he ducked in through the side door to the blessed relief of still air and a modicum of warmth, slamming the door behind him.

"Bit rough, Geoff," he said cheerfully as he joined his colleague at the desk with the panoramic view. "Even the golfers up at Nanpean have called it a day."

The golf course over the old Nanpean fields behind the Cape had manicured the landscape in recent years; the clubhouse a little incongruous from this angle, a plain and rather gaunt granite-faced range of former cattle sheds barely separated from the adjoining old farmhouse, equally ugly in dull painted cement render.

"Thirty-eight miles per hour, gusting forty-five, according to the anemometer," replied Geoff. "The Met reckons it will ease off to twenty-five late afternoon. Could be worse."

"All quiet on the Western Front?" Petroc inquired, glancing at the logbook on the desk. No warnings or emergencies.

"Yep; rather a dull morning, really," Geoff yawned. He stretched and then began gathering his things together into the rucksack hanging on the back of his chair. "One very large container vessel heading north right out on the horizon about an hour ago; otherwise, nothing." He got up to go, dragging on his anorak over his Coastwatch jersey. "Over to you, then. See you, boy."

And he was gone, leaving Petroc alone on lookout duty for his afternoon watch.

Like all his colleagues, Petroc was a volunteer coastguard Watchkeeper with the charity that now undertook this vital task, the professionals having long since withdrawn from that role around the coast of Britain. He enjoyed the work. The solitude, the concentration of purpose, the cosy insulation from the raging elements beyond the windows, the incomparable view, and indeed the occasional walker knocking on the door, curious to know what the work entailed.

Petroc came from an old St Just family, for generations engaged in small-time farming, fishing, building, shopkeeping and mining, some of his forebears carrying on several of these activities at the same time; not unusual in West Cornwall.

For many years he and his wife Jill had run a bed-and-breakfast business in their home, but they were now retired. They still rattled around in their large, comfortable villa in South Place overlooking the Rec. Jill's parents had lived there, as had her paternal grandparents, who had bought it brand new when times were good, financed with a private mortgage from a fellow St Juster. That had been an era in which several scions of local families had shed their meagre inheritance to seek and gain a fortune (relatively speaking) elsewhere, but never shedding their allegiance. They had returned to make their mark in the building of grand homes, Francis Oats of Porthledden being the notable example at the Cape; or to contribute rather more circumspectly to the well-being of the local economy. Jill's great-grandfather had been an agricultural merchant. He had exercised generosity and patience in his credit terms with the family who had then farmed at Nanpean. Gratitude had been expressed by the following generation, hence the Tomlyns' spacious home in South Place. That was how things worked in those days.

Petroc swung the heavy Leviathan binoculars on their fixed stanchion on the desk and slowly scanned the seascape from south to north. Unsurprisingly, there were no vessels in sight. A smudge of grey smoke way off beyond the Longships might mark a big tanker still over the horizon, but equally could be a smear of rain cloud.

The sky was reasonably clear, but for the immediate salt spray. Streaks of very high cloud muted the sunshine in an otherwise blue-grey canopy overhead on this late April day. Out of sight behind him, the half-dozen open fishing boats of Priest's Cove were hauled well up the concrete slipway, linked firmly to their great iron ground chain. None of them would be venturing out for a day or so.

Herring gulls and common gulls flew about out towards the Brisons, forever stalling against the invisible wall of west wind and being carried away only to try again and again, wheeling and crying in their raucous, harsh calls, forever seeking edible flotsam or jetsam thrown up by the waves onto the rocks and shoreline.

The Brisons. Those two incongruous black granite protrusions from the seabed, one a pyramid in shape from this angle, with a heavy dusting of white guano like two sugared Christmas puddings, the last residue of a long finger of rocky landscape pointing out from the coastline south beyond Progo. They were precisely one mile from Petroc's binoculars, but looked closer. Sometimes they looked deceptively close; in other atmospheric conditions, much further away. To frequent viewers the Brisons appeared to be somehow loose from their moorings, drifting in and out at whim from one day to the next.

The VHF radio on the wall behind Petroc crackled briefly. Channel 16 was kept open all the time in order to pick up any calls from vessels within range, in case of 'Mayday' or 'Pan' appeals. Usually it was just for a Channel 65 message from a big-ship skipper or, in high summer, yachtsmen calling for directions into moorings in Penzance or St Ives. Coastwatch was not just a listening ear; it was up to the professionals, the Maritime and Coastguard Agency coastguard bases, however, to cope with emergency calls.

Several times since Petroc had joined the Coastwatch team he had witnessed (and on one occasion had himself alerted) boats in distress along 'his' stretch of coastline and being assisted by the lifeboat from Sennen Cove, only minutes away to the south near the Land's End. Sometimes only the little D Class rigid inflatable boat is needed, perhaps to pick up a capsized canoeist blown out to sea, or a stranded swimmer; but the impressive stuff is handled by the mighty resources of the Tamar Class boat, shot dramatically from her boathouse and down its greased slide with a splash into the water, then powering away to her rescue mission often in sea states far worse than today's.

On this occasion, however, Channel 16 and others were unforthcoming. A few more crackles, a far-distant voice momentarily come and gone with no discernible meaning, and then silence. Not an uncommon occurrence. Petroc just noted it in the log against the time: 1320. He ate his sandwich and drank tea from his Thermos. One corner of the plate-glass observation-window frame was leaking slightly; a dribble or two of salt water running hesitantly down the inner face of the glass onto the desk. He would take a look at that in better, dry weather, armed with a Stanley knife and sealant gun. He was good at that sort of thing.

Mid afternoon, ten past three; 1510. The tide had just turned. The wave pattern had reached its high-tide saturation, the depth of water at the land face swallowing much of the breakers' intensity and explosive effect. These would resume for a while when the tide dropped a little, and then gradually diminish as the ebb began to accelerate. By low tide this evening, just after dusk, the raging would be done. If the wind did continue to drop, tomorrow would be a calmer outlook, with a bit of luck.

Meanwhile, the sea state out beyond the rollers and breakers was still mountainous. Rows of rounded ridges, separated by lines of deep valleys in dark shadow, marched on inwards, a ridge here and there occasionally snarling viciously, its wicked white teeth momentarily showing through parted lips in a spittled grin. (The term 'white horses' hardly does justice to these conditions.) The wind strummed endlessly on a single note through the cable stays of the flagpole that was shackled to the corners of the hut's roof. The sound was amplified through the structure just like the sounding board and body of an acoustic guitar. It could get on one's nerves.

Twenty to six; 1740. The tide was falling fast now, exposing more black rock around the base of the Cape. Great fronds of uprooted wrack lay strewn over the glistening granite, thrown high in the spray to disintegrate into small pieces scattered over the surface of the water, black and shiny.

One particularly large sheet of wrack caught Petroc's eye, draped over a flat rock straight down in front of the lookout hut, now just clear of the diminishing wave surge. He upended the Leviathan on its stand to get a closer look, but it was too steep an angle. He reached for his portable binoculars and adjusted the focus. That was no piece of seaweed. It was a large, ripped sheet of plastic material of some kind; perhaps a sack, or the remains of a cheap tarpaulin. Nothing particularly unusual. Jetsam from freighter traffic often littered the shoreline; these days inevitably some artefact of plastic or another man-made fibre. Usually drinks bottles, snapped cordage, or fish boxes; very occasionally a metal canister of some toxic substance. Anything like that had, of course, to be reported to the MCA or the Environment Agency. Hardly worth recording a sheet of black plastic in the log, although there was nothing much else to do. Petroc would go off watch at seven o'clock, and he was getting just a little bit bored.

The westerly sun was glinting palely now in the windows of the cottages and cafes lining the seafront behind the beach of

Sennen away to the south. The shadows from the rock outcrops on the Cape around the hut were lengthening. Petroc thought with satisfaction of the supper that Jill was no doubt preparing for his return home at about half past seven.Only a quarter of an hour to go now; 1845. He started clearing up the desk. The valuable stuff would be put away in a locked cabinet well out of sight of casual temptation peering in through the windows when no one was on duty. They had suffered a break-in only a few months before, but nothing had been taken. Kids, probably. The hut was not exactly tamper-proof.

The wind had suddenly dropped away, as it often did before dusk. The tide was well down too, the swell still swirling in and around the newly emerging black rocks, eddying in a rather oilier fashion than the more dramatic display of spray and power a few hours previously.

Petroc struggled into his waterproof jacket and swung his rucksack onto his back. Locking the side door behind him, he descended the stone steps and walked back past the old counting house, up the slope towards the car park.

CHAPTER
TWO

PETROC PAUSED AT THE TOP OF THE IMPOSING FLIGHT of chiselled granite steps that led down to the path towards the slipway in the Cove. He often liked to give a last glance out to sea and the Brisons before heading inland and home.

This evening, as he was about to resume his stroll to the car, his attention was drawn to the little tidal seawater swimming pool beyond the slipway. This was a favourite place for children in the summer; safe, but deep enough to swim in. Its perimeter wall had been repaired a few years earlier. What the pool had originally been intended for, Petroc did not know. Perhaps the fishermen had constructed it as a holding tank for live lobsters they had caught. The water in it was constantly renewed because it became completely submerged under the waves at every high tide.

What attracted Petroc's attention this evening was something pale and rounded, floating half submerged in the centre of the pool.

He glanced at his watch. He was hungry and looking forward to his supper, which even now was likely to be reaching peak condition in the oven. No one else was around. His was now the only car left in the car park. The slipway with its multicoloured open fishing boats was deserted.

More flotsam or jetsam, he supposed. But it looked incongruous. He was conscious of his blue Coastwatch jersey underneath his jacket. He was present in an official capacity.

With a short sigh, he turned briskly down the steps and onto the slipway, then jumped down onto the smooth boulders. With the confidence and balance born of much practice, Petroc leapt from stone to stone onto the bedrock in which the swimming pool had been built. He ran along the flat perimeter wall and stared down at the object floating in the dark water.

It was a bloated human body. Shreds of trailing weed clung to it, and it was bereft of all decency.

Petroc had seen a dead body thrown up by the sea once before. The Royal National Lifeboat Institution had found it off the Longships. They had said it had probably only been in the water for thirty-six hours, but already it was disintegrating and partially eaten by sea life.

He immediately noticed the difference with this cadaver. It was still entirely sound and undamaged, except that it had inflated with gases. It was a male; white, and probably in his late forties.

Another sigh, much longer this time, as Petroc stood there contemplating the tragic scene before him. Well, the best thing to do would be to run back up to the Coastwatch hut and alert the coastguard and police from there, using the equipment installed for that very purpose.

He scrambled back up onto the gravel driveway and jogged back around to the west face of the Cape and up the steep steps. Instantly, his memory clicked into place and a connection lodged in his mind. He leant over the parapet of the substantial wall that contained the path from the edge of the vertical abyss to the sea, and peered out onto the exposed rocks below, searching for one in particular.

There. The flat one now high and dry off to his right. And there, too, the odd sheet of black material that he had spotted earlier. He was much closer now, and could see that the object had straps along each side, and a broken zipped flap. It resembled one of those bags that protect a suit from the dry-cleaners, but much longer and heavier.

Of course. Two and two make four. This was a body bag. The body it had lost was presumably the one around the corner bobbing gently in the swimming pool, having been deposited there in the rough sea conditions at high tide.

Petroc strode two steps at a time up the hill and reopened the lookout station. There was a fixed routine for reporting such disasters, and he followed it meticulously. He could safely leave it to the police now. He phoned Jill from his mobile and explained why he was going to be late for supper. Having entered his discoveries in the log, he once again locked up and retraced his steps.

The body bag should be recovered, he realised. It was now nearly eight o'clock, and the tide would turn in an hour. The bag had to be secured before the water rose and carried it away. It was also dusk. The light was failing fast. The job would be impossible in the dark. Goodness knows when the police or the MCA could get here with all their equipment and safety regulations. If the body bag was to be obtained, it was now or never. But could he reach that rock? He leaned over the parapet of the wall, trying to work out a route. If he worked his way round the Cape northwards he thought he could scramble down closer to sea level. There was no way he could descend the vertical side of the abyss from where he was at present.

He put his rucksack on properly, and congratulated himself that it contained a torch. In ten minutes he was down at a level broadly equivalent to the flat rock he was aiming for. But between him and it, the access looked next to impossible. Most of the rock formation, geologically at the junction between granite to the east and slate '*killas*' greenstone to the west, consisted of island-like edifices with sheer sides, individually surrounded by water even at low tide. If he was going to reach that rock, he would have to get wet. Whether this meant wading or swimming remained to be seen.

He quickly discarded his heavy jacket, trousers and boots, leaving them in a prominent position so that he might return to collect them without too much difficulty. Hitching his waterproof rucksack as high on his back as possible, he gingerly set out down the smooth face of a sloping rock to water level.

Beneath the surface, now at dead low water, lay rocks and boulders which never dried out and which were consequently richly coated in slippery green weed. From bitter experience Petroc knew that it was too hazardous to try and balance upright on two feet and attempt to wade from one peak to the next. That was the quickest way to break an ankle.

As that thought passed through his mind, he dug out his mobile phone from a side pocket of his rucksack. No signal. He was too low, and blanketed by the Cape and adjacent cliffs. *Damn.*

He pressed on, crossing small boulders crabwise on all fours, arms and legs underwater. A huge rock island lay in his path which had to be scaled. He reached the top, and there, on the next great slab beyond another stretch of water, lay the shiny black body bag, clearly wedged into a crevice at one corner. Down the other side he climbed, and got halfway. Then he lost his footing and scraped a layer of skin off his left leg, shin and thigh, as he dropped to the base into three feet of water. The salt stung, and Petroc winced. Then the same technique through the water towards his goal, on all fours and scrabbling over rounded boulders laden with dense, treacherous green weed. He slid and skidded from one stone to the next, rubbing both elbows and knees raw with the constant slippage.

At last he was able to grasp the lip of the big flat rock and haul himself up over the rim onto the natural platform above. He looked back at the way he had come. It was rapidly growing dark now, and he could barely make out the shoreline. He consulted his watch and then swore softly to himself. Of course, his watch had stopped, having been immersed several times in seawater. What a fool. Why hadn't he thought to put it in his rucksack?

Anyway, here was the body bag. He jerked the trapped strap buckle out of the crevice and tried to roll the bag up as tightly as he could. He remembered the dog lead in his rucksack, and used it to tie the roll up securely.

As he was doing so, something metallic fell out of the bag and clattered onto the rocky platform at his feet. It was a small aluminium plate or tag, like a label of some kind. He picked it up and scrutinised it a bit more closely. The remains of a cord knot were threaded through a hole at one end. The face of the tag was indented with figures; clearly it was some form of identification. 'AL6043/18' in clear capitals; then beneath that, in smaller lettering, 'Lnne VD CHUV'.

Petroc stuffed it into his rucksack, then turned back towards the land to survey his route back to the shore. It was decidedly dimpsy by now; dark enough to obscure his point of departure. He could no longer make out his pile of clothing, but no matter – all he had to do was retrace his steps.

He scrambled down off the flat rock and began to wade and crawl across to the next crag, the seawater once more stinging his flayed and bleeding leg. Suddenly he was up to his chest in water. Of course – the tide had turned, and was now creeping with silent fingers into all the shallow spaces and crannies that he had earlier negotiated.

He had the presence of mind to flip his rucksack over his head and then adjust the straps so that it hung high and reasonably dry around his neck. He was beginning to shiver now. The water was intensely cold, and being half in and half out in the chill breeze made the effect on his body all the more severe.

With a combination of foot-slithering and encumbered breaststroke, he reached the intermediate rock and hauled himself out, over the top and down the other side. Only one more stretch of water to cross and he could then clamber up to safety. This stretch was deeper. He tried holding the rucksack on top of his head like an African water carrier. Balance was tricky, but at least he could walk upright on the submerged boulders, as the depth of water held him vertical.

But where the heck was the crevice in the shoreline rock face that he had climbed down originally? He must, he supposed, be approaching from a different angle to the one he had used when setting out. It was really quite dark now. With care, he dug around in the rucksack with his hand over his head to find the torch. In the process he nearly lost the rolled-up body bag from under his other arm. It fell with a splash and sank, but mercifully was not carried away in the strengthening eddy of the tide. Petroc trod on it to hold it still and turned his attention back to his escape route, scanning the rocks with the torch in his teeth. There – away to the left. He had come much too far round south of his starting point.

With his little torch clamped in his aching jaw, he trudged around the base of the black wall of granite, and there, perched up above, lay his pile of clothing. In his relief his jaw muscles slackened, and his torch dropped to the seabed. No matter; he had found his route home. Flinging his rucksack up onto the first ledge, he hauled the body bag up out of the water.

He was now very cold indeed, but sensibly made no attempt to remove his wet shirt and underclothes. He rapidly donned his dry trousers, jersey and anorak, slipped on his boots, and plodded with his arms full back up the steps to the Coastwatch station. Out of breath, but more warmly damp, he found his keys and entered the welcome shelter of the hut.

A couple of phone calls, firstly to Jill and then to the police, and Petroc felt that he had rather earned his supper. Locking up again, he trudged back to his car with his rucksack and the body bag.

There was no sign of police or anyone else in the Cove. The tide had not yet reached the swimming pool, but it was too dark to see if there was anything still in it. Presumably the police had come, and gone away with the body. Petroc was past caring. He drove home, squelching warmly with every movement in the car seat.

CHAPTER
THREE

A FTER A BATH AND A CHANGE OF CLOTHES, AND A much anticipated late supper reheated by the solicitous Jill, Petroc drove into Penzance to deliver the body bag to the police station. He spoke to the duty sergeant and reported a brief, edited version of his recovery of the bag off the rock, and left it at that. He understood that in due course a formal statement might be needed.

His mind on other pressing domestic matters (not least a glitch with his bank overdraft), Petroc bought what he needed at Morrisons, and returned home to St Just and bed.

It was a couple of days later, as he once again resumed his watchkeeper duty on the Cape, that he drew that morning's edition of *The Cornishman* out of his rucksack at lunchtime, leaving Geoff to maintain lookout. It was all there on the front page, of course: the body so far unidentified; the discovery by Mr Petroc Tomlyn of St Just; the body bag presumed to be linked to the corpse but offering no clues beyond the fact that, apparently, it was of Swiss manufacture (all too often needed in that country for mountaineering fatalities). The hospital mortuary in Truro, where the body had been taken for analysis, was reported to have concluded that it had defrosted while in the sea, implying that it may have been deep-frozen on a ship from goodness knows where.

Petroc dug further into his bag for his sandwiches and suddenly felt, amongst the string and assorted debris in its depths, a sharp, flat object, which he drew out for examination. Instantly he recognised it as the aluminium tag from the body bag. He had completely forgotten its existence. The tortuous and slightly alarming scramble in the dark, back through the water and over the rocks, had dismissed the discovery from his mind, and the delivery of the body bag to the police station had been so waylaid by his exhaustion and other concerns at the time that he had entirely overlooked the little scrap of metal that he had thrust unthinkingly into his rucksack.

Months later, Petroc was to recall this moment as the pivot on which balanced his humdrum, routine life on the one hand; and on the other, the novel, alarming and dangerous role which was shortly to unfold.

It was, of course, highly irresponsible. Had he instinctively leant towards duty and routine, he would have taken the little tag to the police station with profuse apologies for having forgotten about it. No doubt the powers that be would have used well-worn channels of inquiry to identify the origin of the tag and thereby solve the mystery.

But some old genetic trace in Petroc's Cornish blood asserted itself in that instant; a spirit of adventure and independence dredged from an ancestry of dangerous living that probably included smuggling as well as fishing and mining off this rocky coast lying before him through the window of the Coastwatch station.

He said nothing to Geoff as he slipped the metallic object back into his rucksack. He would launch his own private investigation into this mystery. A slight shiver of shame and excitement ran down his spine. Maybe he could beat the experts at their own game. Shades of his forebears outwitting the Excise men over barrels of French brandy silently applauded from across the past three centuries. Petroc smiled wickedly to himself.

*

Back home in his study, he examined the piece of aluminium more closely under the desk lamp. A rectangle with the corners rounded off, about an inch-and-a-half by three-quarters of an inch, a hole punched in one end. The letters and numbers were also punched in, leaving a raised effect like embossed writing paper.

'AL6043/18'. Obviously a reference number, perhaps relating to the storage facility where the corpse had been frozen. '18' might refer to the current year, 2018. But 'Lnne VD CHUV'? A clinic, perhaps. 'VD' – surely not venereal disease, but if so then it must be of British origin, or at least from an English-speaking country.

'Lnne'. Not a word in itself; an extra vowel or two were needed. It was not in capitals, so couldn't be an acronym. Maybe an abbreviation of some kind? Lorraine? No, there were two 'n's. Something '–nine'? Leonine? More likely to be a noun than an adjective, though. Of course – what about a place name? That would make much more sense. The town or city where the freezer storage was located. Now Petroc knew he was on to something.

He jumped up and went to his bookshelves to find his *AA Book of the Road*. He ran his finger down the gazetteer index at the back. Six possibilities from Langstone to Linkinhorne to Longstone, including Lindisfarne. All equally unlikely.

But what about much further afield? He searched around his shelves for the battered world atlas he still kept somewhere from his early schooldays. After a hunt, he found it buried under a stack of old gardening magazines, and blew off the dust. He flipped through it with a nostalgic smile. Most of the countries seemed to be colour-washed in pale pink; the heritage of the British Empire still prevalent in his youth. Cities and larger towns were listed at the back in a modest index. There were, surprisingly, only two entries that met the likely criteria. Les Sables-d'Olonne in France was one. The other was Lausanne in Switzerland.

Switzerland! Of course, Petroc thought to himself, *how silly. A fine detective you will make, I don't think.* The body bag was stated to be of Swiss manufacture. He knew that already. He must sharpen up his wits if he was going to beat the professionals at this game.

Lausanne. North shore of Lac Léman, east of Geneva. He found it on the map of Europe.

Now, Petroc had recently seen a full-page colour advertisement in the Saturday supplement of his daily paper depicting the attractions of the Swiss lakes. Intense blue water, quaint old buildings, and a backcloth of snow-capped and pine-laden mountains.

He closed the atlas thoughtfully.

CHAPTER
FOUR

"JILL," SAID PETROC OVER THE BREAKFAST TABLE THE following morning, "what do you say to a late spring holiday? We've not been away for ages."

Jill looked up, surprised. Her husband was right – they had not been away from West Cornwall for ages, but this was entirely due to the fact that Petroc was never interested in going anywhere. She looked at him askance. "When you say, 'away', love, do you have in mind another trip to Falmouth, or were you thinking of something east of the Tamar?"

A pause, during which Petroc spread his toast with marmalade. "Well, no, actually. I was thinking more of somewhere considerably further south." He took a bite, and smiled mischievously at his wife.

"What, Guernsey again?" They had been there for their honeymoon. "That would be lovely," Jill hazarded.

"How about Switzerland? You know, cowbells, edelweiss and alpenhorn," he responded.

Jill's eyes opened wide, amazement spreading across her face as she stared at her husband. Then slowly her eyes narrowed, her eyebrows cocked quizzically and she looked at him over her glasses. She knew Petroc all too well. Something was up. "Switzerland. Come on then, you'd better tell me all about it, darling. It sounds wonderful and I can't wait, but why the sudden enthusiasm? We don't ski, and anyway, the snow has long gone. Are we opening a bank account in Zurich, or have you got a new job with the Red Cross in Geneva? I think you had better come clean."

Petroc looked sheepish and took another bite of toast. "Well, yes, I do have a particular reason. How did you guess?"

Jill cast her eyes heavenwards.

"Um, the thing is this, you see," he continued, abashed. "You know that body I found in Priest's Cove? It's a mystery, and, well, I thought it would be rather fun to do some detective work myself. After all, I went to great lengths to salvage the only piece of supporting evidence: that body bag. If it hadn't been for me they would have nothing to go on at all. Anyway, the point is, the bag was made by a Swiss manufacturer."

"So," acknowledged Jill sceptically, "we travel around the country asking if anyone is missing a body bag. How long were you planning to be out there?"

"I've been meaning to tell you. I have another bit of evidence that can home us in on a particular place – Lausanne on Lac Léman, or Lake Geneva. I found it near the bag, but forgot all about it until yesterday." Petroc took the metal tag from his pocket and handed it across the table. "My theory is that 'Lnne' stands for Lausanne. What the rest of it means, I have no idea."

"But, darling," Jill replied anxiously, "shouldn't you be handing this in to the police?"

A long, embarrassed silence.

"Well... yes, I know I really ought to. I just thought it would be quite exciting to beat them at their own game, and do my own sleuthing."

"Petroc Tomlyn, you really are the limit. I mean, think about it. Suppose you are right and this leads to confirmation that the body came from Lausanne. You go to the police, proudly presenting your evidence and telling them you've solved their mystery for them. What will they do? They'll arrest you for something – I dunno – obstructing the police in the execution of their duty, or perverting the course of justice or some such."

Petroc pursed his lips and scratched his head. He sighed. "Suppose so. I just thought it would be rather fun." He thought for a moment. "We could still go out there and see if we can work out the meaning of the tag inscriptions. After all, the police might never release all the details to the press, so we would still need to do our own detective work. And have a good holiday, of course," he added hastily. "OK. I'll take the tag in to the police in PZ this afternoon. I'm on duty at the Cape this morning."

But events were not to pan out quite as he had anticipated.

CHAPTER
FIVE

THE READERSHIP OF *THE CORNISHMAN* IS BY NO MEANS confined to the residents of Cornwall. Other eyes had seen the previous day's report of the washed-up body and the Swiss body bag.

One pair of sharp eyes in particular, in a certain embassy in Holland Park, London, had read it impassively save for the twitch of an eyebrow. Their owner had reached for his mobile phone and issued peremptory instructions, in a language that was not English.

Further instructions had led to an addition to the A30 traffic of a fast but nondescript BMW with two occupants heading west, early on the following morning. Discreet inquiries through the press (the London papers having now picked up the Cornish story) had confirmed to their boss that the police had made no further progress with the identification of the body. His overwhelming desire was that this should remain the case permanently.

There were two aspects to the matter that caused him some concern. One was that a post-mortem might be overzealous and reveal an underlying characteristic that could prove awkward. The other was that this local fellow from the coastal lookout who had discovered the body, and the bag, might have registered certain other features of the incident that had not as yet been reported. He could, for instance, have noted in his logbook a passing vessel from which to make a connection; or perhaps some other detail that compromised the situation. That risk had to be eliminated.

The driver of the BMW was in a black mood. He was out of his comfort zone in deep countryside. It made him nervous. City streets were so much more predictable, ordered and well lit. He had scraped the side of the passenger door along a protruding granite ledge stone on the narrow, twisting lane down to Cape Cornwall, driving too fast around a corner and meeting a delivery van that was leaving the golf club premises. He had tried to squeeze through to save face, as his ability to reverse was limited to street parking. The van driver had sat there with folded arms and a sarcastic expression while he then attempted to back up fifteen yards into a gateway, cracking his nearside brake light on the stone gatepost.

To add insult to injury, he then had to pay cash to park in the field. (He was not a member of the National Trust.) By the time he and his companion were trudging down the road to the Cape, they were both thoroughly fed up. It was raining now, with that true wetness that results from horizontal rainfall in a strong onshore breeze. They had no mackintoshes, and were shod in thin leather-soled town shoes.

This Petroc Tomlyn person they were looking for had better co-operate, they both thought grimly to themselves. They did not have his home address; only the location of the Coastwatch station. He may or may not be there, but at least they could make inquiries.

Both men were English and had been issued with identity cards purporting to represent the Metropolitan Police. This was a familiar disguise in their profession. They had other convenient identities to call upon, but this seemed the most appropriate for the current mission. In the time available it had not been practicable to produce fake warrant cards for the Devon and Cornwall Constabulary.

This morning they were, of course, in luck. Petroc had himself only reached the lookout hut half an hour before their arrival. He had poured himself his first cup of Thermos tea when, rather short of breath and very damp, they knocked on the door.

"Mr Petroc Tomlyn?" the BMW driver asked, masking his Cockney accent as best he could. "Might we have a word, sir?"

The man's colleague, Petroc noticed, hovered outside for a moment, looking around for any other signs of life, before also entering the hut and closing the door. They showed their warrant cards.

"We are following up preliminary inquiries by our Cornish colleagues," the driver continued, "in the case of the body of the deceased male which you discovered near here recently. His identity remains unknown, and we would appreciate your time to answer a few questions in case you can assist us further."

Petroc's heart missed a beat. *Do they already suspect that I am withholding evidence?* he thought with alarm. *If only I had handed that tag in at Penzance before these officers arrived. What do I do now?* "Of course, Officer," he replied with a forced smile. "How can I help?"

"We would like to see the log for the day in question, and the two previous days. It is possible that recorded vessel traffic passing in either direction could give us a pointer."

"By all means," said Petroc with some relief, "but the Penzance police have already looked at that."

"Ah... well, sir, you see, our inquiries may extend further than those of the local force. Up in London, you understand."

(*Oop Lunnon towne*, Petroc thought to himself. *As if I don't know where that is. What do they take me for?*)

The men duly wrote a note of all sightings in the logbook.

"Now, sir, is there anything else you can remember about the body or the body bag that you believe may be helpful?"

"Well," Petroc began cautiously, "the body was naked, so no clues there. It wasn't anybody I recognised," he joked, with an attempt at bonhomie.

Neither of his visitors smiled.

Then the BMW driver asked the question uppermost in his employer's anxious mind – indeed, the only question that had motivated him to dispatch these men to the Cape at all. "Are you quite sure, sir, that there was nothing at all inside the body bag when you found it?"

Petroc swallowed nervously. Should he own up now, or leave it till later? He glanced at his interlocutor. This officer was from the Met. Surely he was senior to the Penzance police. If he did not come clean now, there could be big trouble later. He tried to look ironic. "You know, Officer, it's extraordinary that you should turn up just now and ask that question. Recovering that bag from the rocks down there," he pointed out of the window at the black base of the Cape, now bursting with salt spray, "was a hazardous job, and what with one thing and another I had completely forgotten about a little object that fell onto the rock when I picked up the bag. It went into my rucksack, and only yesterday I came across it again. I was going to take it along to the police station this afternoon."

(Such had been his prepared speech for the benefit of the Penzance inspector.) He dug in his pocket and drew out the little aluminium tag. He handed it over, slightly taken aback at the way it was snatched from him, glanced at and pocketed by the man in the damp suit.

"Thank you, sir," the man said, looking meaningfully over Petroc's head at his colleague. "We can take care of this item now. No need to bother the Penzance police at all. We really are much obliged. This might well assist us in our inquiries. Just one more question." And here he almost imperceptibly nodded to his accomplice, who moved slightly to block the doorway. "I don't suppose you took much notice of what is written on that little label, did you, sir?"

Petroc somehow felt that a blatant untruth at this point might be prudent. "Lord, no," he replied casually. "I looked at it, of course, but it was totally meaningless to me. Anyway, I was slithering around on the rock and anxious to get back to the shore. I never gave it another thought. I assume it's some kind of identity tag, either for the bag or the corpse. I hope you can make head or tail of it."

The man studied his face, clearly weighing something up in his mind. His colleague, standing behind Petroc, eased his right hand silently inside his jacket below his armpit.

"I expect we will, sir. Can you remember if... erm... say, any of the figures on it matched anything printed on the body bag, for instance?"

Petroc was in his stride now. "I've no idea what the tag has written on it, I'm afraid. And I didn't notice anything printed on the bag; certainly on the outside. I never looked inside – possibly there is a label in it somewhere. Not the sort of thing I'm any good at. Sorry," he added for good measure.

The man glanced again at his colleague, who shrugged his shoulders and quickly shook his head. Three seconds passed, and the man visibly relaxed. "Most grateful, sir. We will take up no more of your time. Just one thing – routine, you understand – please do not mention our visit or our conversation to anyone at all. It could compromise the investigation."

With that, both men departed the building, back into the driving drizzle, and descended the stone steps.

Petroc watched them through the window. *An odd pair*, he thought; *not quite my idea of London detectives, but there we are. What do I know?*

CHAPTER
SIX

PETROC RETURNED HOME IN THE EARLY AFTERNOON TO find Jill planting seeds in the vegetable garden. He wandered out to join her.

"Problem solved," he called cheerfully. "The Met sent two officers to the Cape to interview me, so I gave them the tag. They were quite happy with my explanation. Poor things, they were very wet by the time they reached the lookout station. Real townies, hopelessly ill-dressed for Cornish cliffs. Anyway, that's that. "Now," he began cautiously as he stood watching his wife lay a row of broad beans, "shall we pursue my idea of a Swiss sleuthing holiday? My conscience is clear, thanks to you. We can just see if we can solve the puzzle while having a good time."

Jill looked up at him and wiped her brow with the back of a muddy hand. Then she smiled. "Well, I have to admit, it would be quite fun. When shall we go?"

"How about the last couple of weeks in May?" he replied.

"Nothing much else on then. I'll look at some websites about the Lausanne area and we can choose somewhere nice to stay. I guess we fly to Geneva, and then there must be trains, or maybe a ferry along the Lake."

*

The two police impersonators reached London in mid afternoon, returning the BMW to the down-at-heel auto engineer's tatty premises on the industrial estate in Brentford from whence it had come. They went their separate ways, merging into the anonymous murk of the capital city, the senior of the two towards an agreed meeting place with his boss from the embassy in a chain cafe at Paddington station.

"Got what yer wanted, chief," he murmured. "Very easy, as luck would 'ave it. Coupla hours later 'n' this would've been in the hands of the Cornwall fuzz." He passed over the aluminium body tag. "You were right. That coast lookout bloke could've made bad trouble."

His boss checked the tag and put it in his pocket. "Did you have to, ah, dispense with the witness? Could be awkward. Too much of a coincidence."

"Nah, chief," was the welcome response. "'E never suspected nuffink. Took us for the Met and 'as no reason ter talk to the Cornwall Poliss. Ah quizzed 'im abaht 'im noticin' any of the numbers on the label. Jacko 'n' me were satisfied he 'adn't clocked any of it. Vague sort of feller, 'e were. You can forget 'im."

"I'm relieved to hear it. You've done well, Coke. Now push off and keep your mouth shut. Remind Jacko to do the same when you pass him this." He handed Coke two fat brown envelopes stuffed with fifty-pound notes. "And make sure he gets the envelope."

"Will do, chief." And with that, Coke was quickly subsumed into the station crowd.

The gentleman from the embassy took another sip of his black americano, screwed up his face in distaste, and abandoned it on the greasy table. Scrupulously wiping his fingers on a paper napkin, he rose and made his way briskly to the taxi rank.

A meeting had been convened near Regent's Park that evening for certain interested parties. He could bring them up to date on the steps he had taken to prevent identity, at any rate. There was not much any of them could do to cope with the other potential issue.

He just hoped that the Truro hospital mortuary staff, and the police forensics people, were being meticulous on one hand, and superficial on the other. Superficial in not delving too deeply into the more interesting possible causes of death; meticulous in observing very strict measures to protect themselves from contamination, maintaining post-mortem hygiene practices to the letter.

He winced at the thought of seeing headlines in the national dailies screaming the news of wildfire viral death amongst medical personnel in a Cornish hospital. The political implications at an international level were not something he cared to brood upon.

The other problem uppermost in his mind was of a more personal nature. At all costs, this little disaster had to be kept scrupulously confidential. If his ambassador or any of his colleagues not involved in this bit of unofficial business ever learnt of the connection between the dead body and some of His Excellency's staff, he would have to make a run for it – and quickly. He had a variety of fake documents, naturally, and could get back onto the continent without difficulty – but where would he go then?

*

Chief Inspector Drury glanced at the clock in the conference room in Truro police station. His meeting had already overrun, but he would go round the table once more, inviting each of his colleagues by name to offer any further thoughts they may have – however tentative or unlikely, inspired or pure guesswork – in an attempt to establish the identity of the defrosted cadaver washed ashore at the Cape.

Time of death had, of course, been impossible to determine. Much like soft fruit, many internal body parts had degraded into a frankly mushy condition. There was no way of knowing how long the corpse had been in a deep freeze.

Forensics had been confident that the body had been frozen very shortly after death. There was no indication of physical injury or abnormality. Death had, in their view, resulted from organ failure, but the essential organs were all decomposed too far to determine which had failed, or why or how.

So far as normal detective work was concerned, five facts were quite clear.

Firstly, the body had become separated from the body bag only a few hours before discovery. Damage from sea life was minimal so far as the skin and external features were concerned.

Secondly, the body had definitely come out of that particular body bag. DNA sampling proved that beyond reasonable doubt.

Thirdly, the bag was not watertight. The material of which it was made was waterproof, but total immersion had let seawater in through the zip fastener and Velcro tabs.

Fourthly, the bag had been manufactured by a company in Zurich which supplied such items widely to armed forces and disaster agencies in a great many countries in Europe.

Lastly, the deceased was male and around fifty years of age, slightly overweight for his height, and of indefinable Middle European extraction.

From what vessel, aircraft or shoreline vehicle the bag and its contents had been ejected into the sea remained a complete mystery.

Only one further suggestion emerged from the chief inspector's round-table invitation. A detective constable asked hesitantly whether the close-up facial photograph taken of the corpse on arrival at the mortuary had been circulated to all health authorities in Europe, seeking assistance with identification.

It was an extremely long shot, particularly as the face was bloated with gaseous emission, but Drury was grateful for anything. He would arrange the necessary inquiries.

CHAPTER
SEVEN

"**D**O WE HAVE TO FLY?" ASKED JILL, AS SHE AND PETROC studied the laptop screen together one evening, looking at websites. They had booked themselves into a charming old family-run hotel in a village between Lausanne and Vevey, right down on the shore below the famous terraces of the Lavaux vineyards that dated back to the 12th century. There was a railway station five minutes' walk up the hill, with a typically efficient and frequent train service west to Lausanne a quarter of an hour away, and east to Vevey, Montreux, and on into German-speaking cantons beyond the Lake. The website photographs showed an idyllic landscape. "You know I don't like aeroplanes and all that airport ghastliness. I suppose it's a bit far to drive?"

"Yes," mused Petroc, "that would be rather hard work. And I'm not sure our old car would be entirely reliable. But we could, of course, go by train. Let's have a look."

He googled train services from London to Lausanne, and

clicked on one that would organise all the tickets in one exercise. Eurostar to Paris Gare du Nord, the TGV from Gare de Lyon to Lausanne, then the Swiss suburban line to Cully. They could leave London at midday and be comfortably in the lakeside hotel by eight o'clock the same evening. Marvellous. Petroc pressed all the right buttons, entered his credit-card number, and sat back.

"All done. No going back now," he laughed, and wrapped an arm around his wife's waist. "Sherlock Holmes and Watson are off to Switzerland."

*

The man from the embassy, who went by the name of Pietr Stetten (although that was no more his real name than any of the others he had used in his colourful – no, murky – career), pondered the situation. His meeting with his associates had not gone well. They represented several different interests; some government sponsored, others independently powerful. They ranged from official State espionage agents to oligarchs who had bullied and suppressed their way into owning strings of Russian industrial smelting works on a grand scale. Actually, in the latter case the meeting had been attended by their UK representatives. It was far too risky to attend in person.

Stetten in the embassy was best placed to coordinate the project, so he was in charge. This also meant that he was handed the blame when the project faltered.

And this latest incident had potentially hit the fan. It could blow open the entire set-up. If the true cause of death was established by the forensic investigation, their scheme would be revealed – and, what's more, would create a major public panic. Establishing the corpse's identity might be a more manageable risk, but now that the identity tag had been retrieved Pietr felt that this was the least of his worries.

Except... he had a nagging anxiety that there remained a weak security link here. That man Tomlyn. He had read the tag. Coke had been confident that he had not memorised it or indeed taken any interest in it, but he had read the tag. The numbers and code letters might have lodged in his subconscious. If the police in Cornwall did question Tomlyn further, might he suddenly be able to recall the details? The freezer storage cabinet number was not a problem; it was 'Lnne VD CHUV' that would give the game away.

Stetten sat at his desk and bit his nails. *And anyway*, he thought angrily to himself, *how the hell did those idiot Barcelona trawlermen manage to lose the body overboard?* Their job was simple, for goodness' sake. All they had needed to do (having been paid handsomely to do it) was to transport the body, in its bag and inside the ice hold, from their home port across Biscay and up the Bristol Channel to Avonmouth to a handover; a passage in familiar waters that they fished regularly.

It could hardly have been an accident. The only conclusion Stetten could think of was that a UK Fisheries Protection vessel had intercepted them for a routine inspection, and the crew had panicked, chucking the bag and corpse over the side when they saw the official battleship-grey vessel approaching at speed. The trawler might even have been doing a spot of fishing en route, which would explain how far east the bag had floated in the tidal current.

At any rate, the trawler had never made port at Avonmouth. Without the body, the skipper must have just shrugged his shoulders and returned to Barcelona. Certainly the boat was well over the horizon from coastguard stations on the western end of the Cornish peninsula.

So, in the meantime, what to do about Tomlyn? Stetten drummed his fingers on the desk and then made up his mind. Jacko and Coke would just have to tail him for a while; watch and note any police contact with him; report back if Tomlyn did anything out of the ordinary.

He lifted the phone. Coke answered.

"Coke, get Jacko and haul yourselves back down to St Just. Find a cheap self-catering flat and tail that fellow you interviewed down there. Be discreet. I want to know of anything he does out of the ordinary, and any visit he might make to the local police, or if they visit him. And for goodness' sake, look the part. Sweater and jeans, boots. Grow a beard if you are capable of it. Blend in. And tell Jacko to do the same. You're there on a fishing holiday. Buy sea-angling equipment. And don't fall off the rocks into the sea. Or if you do, please drown. I don't want any rescue headlines in the local rag. Just keep your heads down."

"Will do, chief," Coke replied, and hung up with a sigh. Back to that damp, windy, dreary old place miles from anywhere. And he hated fish, except in batter. One end of a fishing rod looked much the same as the other, as far as he was concerned.

He called his mate Jacko and searched around for a suitable holiday-let website for St Just; then he phoned the garage in Brentford. Coke had a hold over the car mender and breaker there, who owed him several favours following a duff deal some years previously. He arranged to pick up a Ford Mondeo the following morning – a car whose back end had certainly not emerged from the Ford factory on the same day, or even the same month, as its front end.

CHAPTER
EIGHT

DCI DRURY SIGNED OFF THE CHIT. IT HAD ALL BEEN most unsatisfactory; the inquest had been given very little to go on and had concluded that the unidentified deceased had died well before entering UK jurisdiction. The evidence of the body bag had indicated that the death had most probably been followed up already by a foreign administration, in which case an inquest had very likely been held by that administration at an earlier date. However, police investigation had failed to identify the country in which death had occurred.

Forensics and the hospital team in Truro had been unable to determine cause of death beyond organ failure, and there was no knowing whether this had been from natural causes. In actual fact, 'unable' was, in the chief inspector's opinion, not entirely accurate. The reality was that the cost of severely limited resources in both the NHS and the Devon and Cornwall Constabulary had not been deemed to warrant exhaustive tests of decayed organ parts in a corpse that had washed up on the Cornish coastline, particularly since no missing person from the UK itself remotely met the physical description of the body, so far as the police were concerned.

With a sigh, Drury handed the signed chit to the constable to take to the morgue. He was releasing the body for cremation. So that was that.

In the meantime, one of the Truro mortuary technicians had gone down with a very bad cold.

*

"He's done what?!" spluttered Pietr Stetten down the telephone. "Are you absolutely certain?"

"Certain damn sure, chief," responded Coke, holding the handset well away from his ear. "'E and 'is missus boarded the Eurostar 'alf an hour ago. They left 'ome in 'oliday gear, carryin' the usual 'oliday stuff."

"Then why the hell aren't you tailing them on the train? Do you know where they're headed? If you lose them, I'll—"

"Relax, chief; I sent Jacko on the train behind 'em. Nah problem, plenty o' seats. He even got the same carriage. It's Paris, not Brussels. 'E'll phone me when Tomlyn and 'is missus change stations, or mebbe stay put in gay Paree. I 'spect they're just off on a bit uv a spring break, like."

"Hmm, well, we will just have to wait and see," replied Stetten, calming down a little. "Phone me the moment you know where they've gone next. Day or night. This is important, Coke, understand me?"

"Understood, chief. Shall I stay 'ere in St Just or return to Lunnon?"

"Stay where you are, Coke. And for God's sake stay within mobile-phone reception. I may need you at short notice."

Stetten put the telephone down and rested his elbows on the desk in front of him. His nerves were playing up badly. He needed to try to relax. Why shouldn't Tomlyn and his wife go to the continent for a holiday? Thousands of people did, every spring and summer.

He picked up once again the published inquest report on the corpse, and read it through for the third time. *Well, that's one thing less to worry about*, he acknowledged to himself. The sooner that body was warm, grey ash and smoke, the happier he would be.

He took a small key from his waistcoat pocket and opened a drawer in his desk. He drew out the little aluminium body tag and gripped it in his fist for the nth time. He returned it carefully and relocked the drawer.

Now all that remained was to prevent or sever any possible connection between that confounded corpse and the establishment on the north shore of Lac Léman in Lausanne, Switzerland.

*

"VD," announced Petroc as he and Jill unpacked their suitcases and put their clothes away in the hotel-room cupboards. "Not a nasty disease, after all. Did you notice the car number plates?" he asked. "I realised as soon as we walked out of the station. They all have 'VD' as part of their number, if they are local. Lausanne is in the canton of Vaud, so the people here are known as the Vaudois. So that solves item two of the body-tag puzzle – I say, that's rather good for our Conan Doyle story: *Sherlock Holmes and the Body-Tag Mystery*. Maybe I'll write this up when we go home."

"Yes, dear," replied Jill, her head in a wardrobe, "but first, I want a nice stroll along the shore of the Lake, followed by a decent dinner in a classy restaurant. That train journey was quite comfortable and quick, but I'm in need of a leg stretch and a good feed."

The weather was warm and the skies a clear, deep blue dome over the Lake, framed to south and east by dark mountains, rock-faced in places and elsewhere bearded with green pinewoods right up to their highest ridges. Some peaks and fissures held the remnants of snow banks, below which narrow waterfalls of immense length fell vertically down the precipitous black mountainsides. It was all too beautiful.

Jill and Petroc sauntered, arm in arm, along the foreshore promenade into Vevey, having taken the train from Cully, only a few minutes' ride away. From Vevey station they had walked down to the shore alongside the ruler-straight, canal-like conduit of the Veneuse river, and joined the throngs of locals and visitors enjoying the evening sunshine. Walking up through the town square, they tried one of the many narrow streets for a promising restaurant, and settled on a pretty corner place with pavement seating. A courteous French waiter took their order and brought them a bottle of the local Corsier Gamay. They relaxed and looked about them. It was all quite delightful.

Jill was roused from her reverie by a sudden exclamation of surprise from Petroc opposite her at the little iron table.

"You know, I'm sure I've seen that chap somewhere before," he said, looking over Jill's shoulder at the people on the pavement on the other side of the street.

Jill looked round.

"That guy with the newspaper in the shop doorway under the Pernod sign. His face is familiar."

Jill followed his gaze. "Hm, no one I know. How funny, coming all this way and spotting someone you know in Cornwall."

"Well, I can't place him," Petroc replied with a frown; "it's just that I'm sure I've met him somewhere. It sort of rings a bell. A rather dimpsy bell, I admit."

"I suppose it's not all that surprising," mused his wife. "There are quite a few English visitors here. I've heard their voices. And Germans – lots of those."

Their conversation was interrupted by the arrival of their waiter, laden with plates and platters of olive breads, dips, oil and hors d'oeuvres. The man with the newspaper was instantly forgotten, and when, after about five minutes, Petroc glanced again across the street, he had gone.

*

Later, much later, as they were sitting, slouched and replete, over their hot, sweet espresso coffee, the shadows had merged into a pale dusk, and a breeze had sprung up from the south, transforming the placid surface of Lake Léman into a frenzy of busy wavelets and, further out, white horses. The little swells were now breaking against the stone promenade wall, sending up white spray which threatened to drench the passers-by.

Jill shivered. "It's cooling off a bit. Let's have a fast walk back up to the station. I'm looking forward to that comfy bed in Cully."

"Tomorrow, let's go into Lausanne and sniff around for clues," suggested Petroc on their return journey.

Jill smiled at him. "Oh, all right. The sooner you can get dead bodies off your chest, the sooner we can relax and be on holiday."

CHAPTER
NINE

"They've gone *where*?!" Stetten spluttered into his telephone.

"Yeah, chief," replied Coke, trying to sound calm but feeling very nervous. His boss was not taking his phone report well. "Jacko phoned me from a place in Switzerland called Vuvee on the edge of some lake. He'd clung to our geezer and his wife like a limpet, and a coupl'a hours ago they were havin' some nosh at a caff in this Vuvee, and then 'eaded to a hotel in a small village nearby called Collie or some such. Jacko 'ad to return to Vuvee to find somewhere to kip for the night, 'cause it was past midnight when 'e phoned me."

Pietr Stetten told Coke to get hold of Jacko and tell him to keep on the Tomlyns' tail, and then hung up. He held his head in his hands, wearily supported on his desk, and tried to think.

This just had to be more than a coincidence. On holiday just a few miles from the one place in Europe whose identity would blow apart the whole project if linked to the body this holidaymaker had himself found only a couple of months ago? It simply wasn't possible.

But what could Stetten do? Arranging for Jacko to intervene physically carried huge risks of exposure. Going to the extreme and killing off the Tomlyns in a secret and convincing manner would be a massive reaction and fraught with problems, not least Jacko. And what if, after all, it *was* an entirely innocent coincidence?

A delaying tactic would help. The fiasco with the Spanish boat crew dumping the body overboard had required urgent work on Stetten's part to find a substitute quickly, to avoid putting the whole project at risk. At his own personal expense he had paid his Lausanne contact to look for another cadaver bearing similar viral-infectious features, and was still trying to organise secure transport, again by ship, to Avonmouth.

The project was now over a month behind schedule, and his powerful colleagues were not the most patient of men.

The extraction and duplication of the virus was to be done in a secret laboratory set up for the purpose in Bristol. Stetten was hazy about the scientific process involved, but was acutely aware of the critical timing. The sponsoring state concerned needed the product by mid July, and in large quantities. Stetten preferred not to dwell too deeply on the consequent implications.

Innocent people in their thousands – even hundreds of thousands – would potentially be sick or dead if the target state chose to resist or defy the ultimatum with which they would be faced at the end of July. That was not Stetten's concern. He had a job to do now, and would just get on with it.

So, in the meantime, if Tomlyn really was foolish enough to stick his nose into this affair and had regrettably made the connection with the Lausanne source, he had to be halted, at least until the end of July. After that, it would no longer matter. Stetten

43

and his associates would by then have obliterated their footprints and disappeared back into the murk – in Stetten's case, probably via a new identity in South America.

He reached for his mobile phone.

*

The mortuary technician in Truro was in bed at home. His wife, a robust midwife at the same hospital, had little sympathy for her husband's regular time off over the years with 'man flu'; but this time she did have to admit that something was genuinely wrong. His temperature was rising and he had a severe headache with muscle pain. She had just found him sitting, shivering, on the lavatory with diarrhoea, and spitting vomit into the adjacent bidet.

*

Petroc and Jill Tomlyn rose the following morning to a bright and sunny view south over Lac Léman. The white paddle steamer *Italie* was making her way elegantly towards the north shore on her way to the jetty at Vevey, streaming her huge red-and-white Swiss ensign off the stern.

They went downstairs to the hotel dining room to be greeted by Madame, and her fair-haired teenage son who did most of the work. Ham, hard-boiled eggs, butter, cheese and croissants were pressed upon them without demur, accompanied by a huge coffee pot and yellow, creamy milk. Copies of the local newspaper in French lay distributed about the room, casually perused by the two or three other occupants who appeared to be familiar locals rather than fellow tourists. Platters heaped with warm croissants lay on several unoccupied tables, evidently available freely to all patrons with the compliments of the management.

Our Cornish couple smiled at one another across the table. This was relaxing. They looked forward to a happy day together ambling around Lausanne, maybe walking up inland into the hills behind that were clothed in deep green pinewoods beyond the bare, stony terraces of the ancient vineyards that faithfully followed the contour lines of the steep slope. Perhaps their sightseeing might prove to have the added spice of a little search for clues in Petroc's pet project to unlock the mystery of 'Lnne VD CHUV'. They were already in 'Lnne VD', but what about 'CHUV'?

After breakfast they gathered what they needed for the day into their small rucksacks and headed for the railway station on the edge of Cully village – in reality, no more than a couple of plain concrete platforms alongside the track. Within ten minutes they were stepping off the train at Lausanne, and walking down the hill towards the lakeside promenade.

Half a dozen other people had alighted from the same train, including a rather thin, saturnine character with the beginnings of a patchy beard. He was dressed, a little incongruously, in clothes reminiscent of an Englishman on a fishing holiday. He kept well behind the Tomlyns, pausing to scan his newspaper (the *Daily Mail*, two days out of date and surprisingly for sale at Vevey station gift shop) whenever Petroc and Jill slowed down to inspect something of interest.

The shoreline of the Lake was attractive, and they wandered along, admiring the very smart yachts and powerboats in the classy marinas. Lausanne was a large conurbation, and much of it rather dull. Jill and Petroc began to tire of the general view, and decided to explore one or two particular landmarks further inland.

By noon they were feeling in need of a sit down and a cup of coffee. In the shade of a white awning over their pavement cafe table, they looked through the various leaflets and guides they had accumulated. La Cathédrale de Lausanne sounded interesting. That was right up in the north of the city towards the rambling campus of the university, shown clearly on their map. It was way up beyond the railway line, and too far to walk with ease.

"Let's get a taxi," Jill suggested. "Then when we've seen the cathedral we could explore further up north into the hills. It looks as though there are some nice countryside walks we could reach. There may be a bus."

They paid the bill and, spotting a taxi rank, set off in that direction.

The English fisherman sitting on a park bench under a plane tree twenty yards away had chosen that moment to buy an ice cream from the bright blue Nestlé kiosk nearby. He turned back to his surveillance duty just as the Tomlyns were getting into their taxi. By the time he had jogged with his dripping ice-cream cone to the taxi rank, they had long since vanished from sight.

Jacko clenched his fists and swore loudly, to the alarm of a mother and child just climbing into the next taxi at the rank. Fortunately the woman did not understand northern Anglo-Saxon, or she would have been highly affronted.

His ice cream toppled out of its cone and landed with a splat on the dusty tarmac. He was not happy.

CHAPTER
TEN

THE CATHEDRAL SOARED OVER THE OLD TOWN AREA OF the city; a vast Gothic structure with, to English eyes, the slightly incongruous feature of both a tower and a spire, one at each end.

As Petroc and Jill entered the building, the organist was practising. The sound was astonishing, and they had difficulty hearing the guide at the door explaining that it was the largest organ in Switzerland – built, needless to say, by an American firm.

After soaking up the atmosphere and admiring the recently revealed ancient wall decorations, they wandered back out into the sunshine.

"Let's carry on up the hill," Jill said.

Before long they found themselves on the long Rue du Bugnon that ran northwards past the hospital; a huge, multilayered modern block that looked like a stack of wafers, surrounded by elegant open spaces and ancillary buildings.

Suddenly Petroc halted on the pavement, Jill cannoning into

him from behind. He turned and looked at his wife, pointing in excitement at a fingerpost sign nearby. "Jill," he exclaimed, his eyes shining, "do you see what I see?"

Jill followed his gaze to the black-and-white road sign, and read it with a puzzled frown. "'*Centre Hospitalier Universitaire Vaudois*'," she read aloud. "Why is that particularly thrilling?"

"Don't you see?" Petroc laughed. "Spell out the first letter of each word. And look, over there, above that open entrance door; that large nameplate. CHUV. The final clue on my body tag. That corpse came from here, right where we're standing."

"All right," answered Jill calmly, "let's go in and take a look around."

They crossed the street and mounted the steps leading into the building. The place was quite busy, with medical staff and what were clearly students mingling with members of the public in the large entrance hall. Everything was sparklingly clean and well ordered, as the Tomlyns had come to expect in the new country they were exploring.

This was clearly one of the main public entrances to the hospital complex. Large signs over the various corridors giving off the hall pointed to different departments. A huge noticeboard on one wall carried a diagrammatic map of the entire complex. They wandered over to look at it more closely. The medical facilities covered a very wide area. Petroc made a mental note of one of them, way up in the north-east of the city in what appeared to be a rural area with woods and absorbing an old village – the Centre for Immunology and Infection in Épalinges.

Then Jill spotted a board which set out some of the history of the hospital, and its specialisms and projects. "Come over here, Petroc," she called over her shoulder. "This looks interesting."

Petroc followed her pointing finger. His French was not good, but he could just about translate the contents of a small explanatory section of print on the noticeboard.

In 2014 Lausanne University Hospital conducted an extensive vaccine trial against the Ebola virus, and continues to lead the way in wider clinical trials of new therapies in defence against some of the world's most intransigent diseases.

Petroc sat down suddenly on one of the bench seats set around the walls of the hospital hallway. He was stunned. "Ebola!" he exclaimed loudly, turning a few nearby heads in his direction.

He and Jill looked at one another in horror.

He lowered his voice. "What the hell is this really all about? What are we getting ourselves into?"

*

Jacko was not entirely unintelligent. He had made a mental note of the taxi that had whisked the Tomlyns away from his surveillance.

He hung around the area of the taxi rank, hoping that it would shortly return, and sure enough, after about twenty minutes the same taxi drew into the rear of the rank.

Jacko wandered over to speak to the driver. He had no French. "*Pardon, mussewer.* Your last passengers are mates of mine an' I just missed contactin' them before they left in your motor. Could you please tell me where you dropped 'em off?"

The taxi driver frowned in concentration, his English being as poor as Jacko's French. "*Quel est 'droptem uff', monsieur? Qu'est-ce que c'est? Le 'mist contact'; c'est un component tombe autour de l'automobile?*" He opened the door of his car and began to walk around it, looking closely at the wing mirrors and hubcaps.

"*Non, non,*" exclaimed Jacko, "*votre* car is fine, nah problem. I just wanted to know where you took yer last passengers – y' know, passargers. They *sont maize ammees.*"

"*Ah, oui, d'accord,*" the driver responded, his face lighting up in understanding. "*Ils sont à la cathédrale.*"

"Cattay Dralay? What is this Cattay?" Jacko asked in frustration. "Oh – Cafe Dralay, d'yer mean? Which cafe is that?"

This conversation could have continued in like manner all afternoon, but the taxi driver pulled out a crumpled old Lausanne street map from the glovebox and pointed a grubby finger at the spot marking Lausanne Cathedral. "*Voici, monsieur. La cathédrale.*"

"Ah, got yer. Thanks, mate." And with that, Jacko ran to the head of the taxi rank and jumped into the black Mercedes cab. "*Cattay draley, seel vouplate.*"

On his arrival, the organist was practising some César Franck, and a number of tourists had sat down in the pews to listen. Jacko peered around over the sea of heads, but there was no sign of the Tomlyns. He hung around outside for a while and then, for want of anything better to do, walked up towards the university campus and the route north-east.

In fact, as it happened, he pretty much followed in the Tomlyns' footsteps, but about half an hour behind them.

His routine call to Coke was long overdue, but he was very reluctant to report in merely to confess that he had lost track of his targets. Jacko reached the Rue du Bugnon and the signage to CHUV and was just about to stroll on up the road when, over to his right, he spotted them. Petroc and Jill were just leaving the hospital entrance. He quickly slipped around the corner of an adjacent building and breathed a sigh of relief, at the same moment bringing up Coke's number on his mobile and making the call.

"That you, mate?" he said fatuously as his call was connected. "Sorry Ah'm late in, but Ah've 'ad a raht job 'ere this afternoon keepin' tabs on ar two jokers."

"You've lost 'em, I suppose," responded Coke with a sarcastic sigh. "Fell asleep in yer deckchair?"

Jacko was roused into justifiable bluster. "Ain't nothin' o' the sort, mate. Ah can see 'em both raht now as we're speakin'. Tell the boss these Tomlyn people 'ave just come art uv the main entrance to a big 'ospital up 'ere norf of the city. It's a place called Centre Hospitaliar Somefink, at the university. The door's got 'chuv' written over the top."

"Chuv?" muttered Coke. "What's 'chuv', then? Well, never mind, I'll just pass on yer message. Just make sure yer don't lose 'em." And he hung up.

*

A quarter of an hour later, Pietr Stetten also slowly replaced his telephone handset on his office desk. He had listened to Coke's report in silence, and indeed had terminated the call without speaking a single word. He slumped back in his leather revolving chair and gazed, unseeing, at the opposite wall of his embassy room, and out of the window onto Holland Park.

He began to think this through. *Try and be logical*, he told himself. *Firstly, the Tomlyns believe that the body tag is in the hands of the Metropolitan Police, and will reasonably assume that they have long since identified the letters and numbers on it. Secondly, the Tomlyns will therefore presume that official contact and investigation have already commenced with the Lausanne University Hospital. And thirdly, they will therefore take it for granted that the significance of the body so far as viral infection is concerned will have already been recognised by the relevant UK authorities, and that the situation is all under official control.*

So far, so good. But in that case, why are these nosy Cornish individuals pursuing their own private detective work?

Two possible reasons occurred to Stetten. First, that they were just doing it for fun, the Tomlyn man having had a personal interest in the matter from the outset of the discovery of the corpse on Cape Cornwall. Second (and this was what prompted Stetten to rise from his chair and pace the room in nervous concentration), perhaps Tomlyn had seen through the impersonation of police officers by Coke and Jacko and believed them to have been impostors – in which case, he would be convinced that he and his wife were the only people who had discovered the meaning of the body tag. At any moment, in that event, they could contact the police and reveal everything. In either scenario, the risk to the project remained a real one.

These Tomlyns had to be stopped.

*

The mortuary technician back in Truro had just been admitted to hospital and was in intensive care. His symptoms were puzzling. His consultant was wondering whether it would be prudent to refer him to a more specialist centre – Southampton, or maybe even the Hospital for Tropical Diseases. His patient's condition seemed to be rooted in a virus that was definitely not indigenous to the British Isles. Of course, the technician's profession laid him open to such wider risks, and inquiries would have to be made. Certainly the man had not travelled overseas recently – if one discounted the Channel Islands, where he and his wife had spent a short winter break.

CHAPTER
ELEVEN

Pietr Stetten faced Coke over the table in a dark corner of The Woolpack pub in Bermondsey Street, almost in the shadow of the great Shard towering over the market and Southwark Cathedral south of the Thames.

"The less you know, the better," Stetten began. "All you need to grasp is that this Tomlyn couple have to be detained, and urgently. You and Jacko have got to find a way of securing them where they are in Switzerland, and holding them until I say otherwise – it could be a couple of months. The vital thing is that they have no means of communication by phone, mail or anything else. And, Coke, no violence. The last thing we need is a complication of that sort. You have to detain them and hold them anonymously, and, when the time comes, to release them without them being able to trace you. Understood?"

"Well, yes, chief," replied Coke doubtfully, "I understand OK, but easier said than done. You're talkin' kidnap, right? Some out-of-the-way place to lock 'em up in; keep 'em fed an' watered 'n' not let anybody else find 'em?"

"You've got it in one," Stetten confirmed with a nod. "How you do it is your affair. All I can do is supply cash. That's on a 'needs must' basis, mind; no extravagances. I'll pay for ordinary accommodation for you and Jacko, but you two must operate a rota for guarding the Tomlyns at all times. And, Coke, keep this strictly to yourselves. I don't want you employing anyone else out there at all. Too risky, see?

"Now, here are airline tickets to Geneva for you this afternoon. Get going, and don't let me down."

"Trust me, chief. I'll do me best."

"Well, you'd better. Stay in touch."

And they each went their separate ways.

*

Petroc and Jill sat on a park bench in one of the many attractive open green spaces around the university campus. Students were sprawled over the warm grass with their books and papers, comparing notes. Lunchtime had come and gone, and the Tomlyns were hungry. They were, however, reluctant to lose their train of thought.

"So," said Jill, "what does it look like? Someone seems to have diverted the dead body of an unfortunate patient from this hospital, presumably by sea, and then either lost or dumped the corpse overboard in the Western Approaches.

"Let's assume what would normally be expected to happen if a patient dies. The body would be released to his or her family, and an undertaker engaged to arrange burial or cremation."

"What if there was no traceable family?" interjected Petroc.

"Well, in that case I guess the hospital or the local authority would arrange for cremation, perhaps with a short ceremony from the hospital chaplain, and the body dealt with at the city crematorium – or possibly the hospital one, if it has such a thing."

"I suppose," pondered Petroc, "that if the deceased was a visitor from Britain, say, then his family might arrange transport back to the UK for burial or cremation in his home town or parish. But surely, in that case – which is not so very unusual – arrangements would be made to fly the body home by plane. There's been nothing in the papers about a plane crash over the Atlantic. Why would the body be brought home slowly by boat? And if it was a commercial ship, surely there would have been a publicised inquiry into the loss of such sensitive cargo? We would have registered anything like that if it had been reported in the papers. We've kept an eye out for media reports on 'our' corpse, but ever since the initial discovery there's been total silence. It's all very odd."

They sat there in their own silence for a minute or two, gazing out over the lower city towards Lac Léman and the snow-capped mountains away to the south.

"OK." Jill broke the silence. "Now, what about these medical experiments into vaccines for Ebola and goodness knows what else? For all we know, this hospital might be investigating cures or therapies for such ghastly things as pulmonary anthrax.

"Now... yes... how's this for a theory? A European man working in the Congo contracts Ebola and is rushed to a clinic there run by Médecins Sans Frontières. This hospital in Switzerland, CHUV, is called in to advise, or at any rate gets to hear of the case. They then arrange to bring the patient back here to care for him and work on his recovery using their specialist research, hopefully to make advances themselves in their treatment trials as well as saving the patient. Then the patient sadly dies. How would the hospital authorities deal with the deceased then?"

"Of course," interrupted Petroc. "They couldn't possibly release the body to an ordinary undertaker or the staff of the town crem. It would be highly dangerous for anyone who came into contact with it – and besides, the hospital would be very anxious to ensure that the death from Ebola, or anthrax, or whatever, did not become public knowledge in and around Lausanne. At the very least, they would have some protocol for safe handling and cremation within tight security on their own premises."

"But what about the family?" queried Jill.

"Well, they would understand, of course, and let the hospital carry on, wouldn't they?"

"All right, so now here's the tricky thing. How come CHUV managed to mislay a high-security corpse? Who got hold of it, and why?"

"And," added Petroc, "did the hospital discover the body's removal? There's no reason to suppose that CHUV and its staff are anything but totally above board and scrupulously professional. But is it possible for someone with criminal intent to purloin – or maybe substitute – a corpse somewhere between the hospital mortuary and crematorium without the staff knowing?"

"We could try and find out," said Jill with a determined glint in her eye. "I'm beginning to realise the implications. Think what widespread havoc could be caused by a criminal organisation being in possession of a corpse riddled with highly infectious Ebola virus. It could hold to ransom anyone it liked."

*

Jacko waited patiently on the station platform for the Geneva train to pull in. He had found cheap bed-and-breakfast accommodation in Lausanne for Coke and himself, above a rather run-down corner cafe well outside the city centre. Both cafe and bedrooms, the latter with tiny en-suite showers, were furnished with shiny laminate wall coverings, cracked ceramic floor tiles of a dull beige colour, and sparse furniture of chrome and plastic. The ubiquitous pale blue Nestlé motif boards were displayed indoors and out at every conceivable opportunity. The whole place was entirely devoid of character or comfort. But it was cheap, impersonal and in the right place. Jacko was pleased with himself.

Later that evening, he and Coke sat uncomfortably at a wobbly steel table in the cafe below their rooms, drinking lager and munching their way through a warm pizza of indeterminate flavour. Other tables were occupied by local Swiss from the surrounding suburbs of nondescript concrete blocks of flats. Spread before Jacko and Coke on the table was a tourist map of the locality at a large scale.

"What we 'ave ter do," said Coke, "is find some out-er-the-way place inland of the town, where we can 'ole up with the Cornish couple without fear of discovery. Now, I've bin thinkin'. Up there in them hills, and further up those mountains, there are marked routes fer cross-country skiing and snow tramping – see these blue lines on the map? I reckon that in the spring an' summer when the snow 'as gorn, these will be little used except fer the more popular paths through the woods for people hikin'. On the back o' this map…" He turned it over, smearing one corner with red pizza sauce. "Damn. Anyway, look, Jacko; yer see this 'ere snowshoe symbol and them little hut signs? These show the positions of small wooden shelters dotted abaht the area, where skiers an' snow walkers can shelter in bad winter weather. It explains 'ere that these huts are kept supplied with logs for their small stoves, an' sometimes basic provisions."

"Yer mean," interrupted Jacko, "we march this geezer 'n' 'is missus up a mountain at gunpoint an' lock 'em up in one of these 'ere cabins; then we feed 'em by pushin' food in through a winder an' keep 'em there for a coupla months? Sounds dodgy, mate."

Coke closed his eyes and counted silently to ten in an effort to remain patient. He was used to doing this when conversing with his colleague. "Not exactly, Jacko. But you've grasped the gen'ral principle. Now shuddup a minute while I study this map."

CHAPTER
TWELVE

THE FOLLOWING DAY, AFTER A LEISURELY BREAKFAST, the Tomlyns sat in the sunshine on the shoreline of Lac Léman watching the beautiful white paddle steamer approach like an elegant swan across the water towards Vevey to the east.

On their return to Cully the previous evening, they had booked a steamer trip on the *Italie* around the lakeside towns to the far eastern end of the valley and round in a clockwise circle to take in the little town of Saint-Gingolph on the south bank, and then back to Vevey. It was the perfect day for the little voyage – not a breath of wind, and a clear sky.

The departure time was twelve noon, and so they took the suburban train over to Vevey and wandered down into the town square, which was bustling with visitors and colour. Near the promenade, a rather striking steel sculpture drew their attention. It was multicoloured, and comprised a tall, spiky edifice constructed of salvaged metal components welded together. Several people were admiring it, and the Tomlyns joined them.

Suddenly, Petroc put his hand on Jill's arm. "There he is again – over there by the Camera Museum. That chap I recognised when we were having supper here. He's looking this way – I think he's spotted me too. I wish I could place him."

"Well," said Jill, "perhaps we should go over and find out who he is."

So they began to walk across the square.

"He's with someone else, I think," Jill continued. "That chap in a dark suit."

Petroc squinted into the sun. "Yes, you're right. Hey, I know him too. Now, where on earth have I seen those two men before?"

"They've seen us and are coming this way," replied Jill. "Maybe they're from Penzance. What a coincidence! I don't suppose they're Coastwatch, are they?"

"Not Coastwatch, no. Gosh – of course, I remember. They are the two policemen who came to see me on the Cape after I found the body. They're from the Met." Petroc laughed. "Well, they would be here, wouldn't they? On the same trail as us!" He strode across with a welcoming smile and put out his hand to the man in the suit. "Hello again. I thought I recognised you."

"Good morning, sir," replied Coke, which was what he thought a Met Police officer would probably say in this situation. "This is a surprise."

Jacko stood behind him, looking suitably solemn, but rather less convincing in his worn jeans and faded guernsey.

"This is my wife, Jill," continued Petroc. "We are here on a bit of a holiday, and are just about to go aboard that steamer for a trip around the Lake. My, it's a small world, isn't it? Cape Cornwall and then Switzerland. I take it you and your colleague are here on police business?" he concluded innocently.

"I'm not in a position ter say, sir," Coke replied, "as I'm sure you will understand."

"Of course, Officer," said Petroc.

There was a slight pause in the conversation.

"Can I ask if you have managed to solve the mystery of that body I discovered washed up in Priest's Cove? We haven't seen anything in the newspapers, but I've been keeping an eye out. It certainly hasn't made the headlines."

"No, sir," replied Coke, "but I shouldn't worry yourself about that. We 'ave the matter well in hand, I can assure you."

The *Italie* was alongside the pier now, her huge paddle wheels idling slowly in the blue water, causing the surface to froth and whiten, lapping gently against the timber pierhead. The first officer and his mate stood at the foot of the ramp to welcome the queue of passengers, immaculate in their smart peaked caps and gold jacket insignia.

Jill took her husband's arm. "Well, I think we had better board the boat, or we will be left behind," she said, with a quick, meaningful glance up into Petroc's eyes. "Very pleased to have met you." She nodded to the two men. "Goodbye."

Coke raised a hand in farewell, and gave Jill a smile. "Good afternoon, ma'am; have a pleasant holiday."

The two men watched the Tomlyns walk up the ramp onto the steamer.

"They're playin' rahht into our 'ands," murmured Coke with satisfaction.

"If yer say so," responded Jacko, who looked as mystified as he felt.

*

"I don't like it," Jill declared firmly, as they took their seats on the slatted bench up in the bows of the vessel, where they would

60

have an excellent view of the scenery, as the steamer moved sedately away from the shore. "They just don't seem right to me. That silent one – he looks underfed, unintelligent and a bit sly. Hardly police officer material, I'd have thought."

"But they showed me their Met ID when they came up to interview me – I remember distinctly, because it was so unexpected." Petroc paused with a frown. "Still, it is a bit odd that they should be right here in Vevey so long after the corpse incident. You'd have thought their investigations would be well beyond Lausanne by now."

"And," interposed Jill, "just at the very moment that you are here. Can it be more than a coincidence, I wonder?"

"Well," objected Petroc, "surely they are not tailing me? I mean, they can't suspect me of having something to do with a plot to contaminate the population with some deadly disease? It doesn't make sense."

They gazed ahead at the glorious vista opening out towards the eastern end of Lac Léman, as they passed close by the high walls of the famous Castle Chillon standing on its rocky island jutting from the shoreline, ancestral and cantonal flags fluttering from their poles on the ramparts. High above and beyond the lakeside township soared the incongruous but impressive white-concrete motorway flyover, perched almost impossibly on its slender pillars several hundred feet above the ground.

Petroc and Jill settled back in their seats to savour their trip around the stunningly beautiful shores of the Lake. Puzzling over the presence of the two police officers could wait. They were here to enjoy themselves. Jill had put together a picnic lunch in her rucksack, and they munched happily as they watched the world go by.

*

Later that afternoon, back in Vevey, they wandered along the promenade, lined with its strangely pollarded plane trees, and sat in the sunshine on a bench to admire the little fleet of lugsail boats that had set out together into the Lake from La Tour-de-Peilz.

Neither of them noticed an unremarkable small grey Citroën van pass slowly along the road behind them, pausing briefly when the driver spotted them and turned his face away before moving on.

The man at the wheel was Coke. He was smiling to himself.

CHAPTER
THIRTEEN

DCI Drury looked up from his desk at Truro police station as he heard a knock on his door and a young detective constable appeared hesitantly in the doorway.

"Come on in, lad," he said encouragingly. "Have you come to brighten up my Monday afternoon?"

"Well, sir," replied the officer, "you remember the case of that washed-up corpse of a male down on Cape Cornwall back along? You asked me to circulate his photograph around the main health authorities in Europe to see if any of their hospital mortuaries might recognise it? Bit of a long shot, but we've had two replies."

"Go on," prompted Drury, as his constable paused.

"Yes, sir, well – one is from Dresden in Germany. They have sent morgue record photos of three males handled early in the New Year. One of them I reckon is a possible match, but our corpse was so bloated in the face that it's very hard to be confident. At any rate, all three were recorded as being cremated on the hospital's own premises in late March."

"And the other?" Drury asked.

"Slightly more promising, sir, for a reason I'll come to in a moment. This is from the University Hospital of Lausanne in Switzerland." The DC handed the chief inspector a monochrome photograph. "Again, the visual image is by no means conclusive, but you'll see from our own photo," and here he produced a copy of the Truro hospital's upper-body photograph of the Cape corpse, "that it could well be the same man.

"Now, there are two interesting bits of possible corroborative evidence that I have noted for you, sir. Firstly, I googled the Lausanne hospital, and read that in 2014 they ran major vaccine experiments for the Ebola virus that you'll remember was breaking out in a big way in Central Africa. In fact, Lausanne University runs similar clinical trials into all sorts of serious diseases from around the world."

"Ebola!" interrupted Drury. "Hmm. Nasty. But what can that possibly have to do with our corpse?"

"Well, sir," and here the young constable's voice suddenly displayed a ring of excitement, "just this morning we have had a report from the hospital in Southampton, passed on to us by the clinical director of Treliske here in Truro. Treliske hospital sent them a patient in a critical condition, who happens to be one of the Treliske mortuary technicians. This guy is just about holding on, but this is the thing, sir – guess what he's been diagnosed with?"

"I don't do guessing games, Constable," growled Drury, "but you're telling me this patient has Ebola, right?"

"Yes, sir – and here's the clincher: he was on duty during the attempted autopsy of our corpse, and became ill shortly afterwards."

Silence pervaded the chief inspector's office for a frozen minute. Drury suddenly stood up and turned to the window, hands clasped behind his back, staring out at the drizzle drifting in from the west. The constable began to wonder if his boss had forgotten that he was still there, but then Drury turned again and resumed his seat.

"Right. First question – has the Lausanne hospital's response included any confirmation of their patient's cremation?"

"Oh – yes, sir; I was going to hand this over as well. Here's their brief report. It explains that the patient had come to them from a place called Lubumbashi in the Congo Republic, where he had been working with the locals as a mining engineer. He had contracted Ebola, and ended up in Lausanne for some experimental treatment. He was too ill to survive, unfortunately.

"Now, sir, here's an interesting thing. For some reason they don't explain, their hospital crematorium was not running at the time, so the body was transferred in a sealed bag to the local authority and cremated..." The DC searched the document with his finger. "Yes, here we are. He was apparently cremated at the Centre Funéraire de Montoie in Lausanne."

"OK," acknowledged Drury with a nod, "so, what if he wasn't? Somewhere along the line between the University Hospital and the local authority crem, according to your theory, the body was diverted."

"Yes, sir, and I think we can safely assume that the body was substituted unofficially for another corpse, because the local crem supplied the hospital with normal documentary confirmation that the disposal was completed."

"Unless, of course," mused Drury, "the document was falsified. But that would mean that a local authority official was complicit in the deception, wouldn't it? Simpler at this stage to work on the basis that there was a substitution by a third party wholly without the knowledge of either hospital or local authority staff. And, presumably again, by a person or persons with criminal intent."

Drury lifted his desk telephone. "Can you get me an appointment with the Super in about an hour's time, please,

Janet? And I want the file on that corpse that was washed up on Cape Cornwall back in April." He looked up at his young colleague and smiled. "Good work, lad. The next thing you can do is look up how we get in touch with our gendarmerie friends in Switzerland. I have a feeling we may need to bone up on our French."

*

Meanwhile, a cloud of despondency was hanging over a certain embassy building away to the east in Holland Park, London. Pietr Stetten had just put the phone down on his compatriot colleague in downtown Lausanne. This man, Willi Valtmeier by name (a pseudonym taken from an unfortunate victim of an over-enthusiastic assault, when Willi had been an agent of the Stasi back in the 1970s), was proving difficult.

He was, he frankly admitted, getting bored. For more than two years now he had been working for Stetten on this project, his task being to secure a suitably large sample of human tissue known to be contaminated with one or other of the deadly contagious or infectious viruses on the list Stetten had supplied for him when he was recruited.

Initially he had infiltrated a large hospital in Salamanca as a mortuary technician, using forged certificates of training and competence. There he had twice succeeded in purloining body parts of autopsied cadavers that had been, respectively, victims of Nipah virus and SARS. Unfortunately, on both occasions, by the time they had reached Stetten's facility in Bristol, they had been found to be inadequate for their purpose. The first delivery had suffered a refrigeration failure en route; the second had been so saturated with medication from earlier attempts by the hospital to save their patient that laboratory isolation of the unadulterated virus had proved ineffective.

Then he had come to Lausanne, and after judicious inquiry had again forged qualification evidence and signed on as an auxiliary ambulance driver for a private German contractor that supplied transport services to medical centres throughout Switzerland, including the CHUV on the shores of Lac Léman.

He had soon struck lucky. He had been on duty with a paramedic colleague only recently engaged by the firm, when they had been instructed to transport a sealed body bag containing an Ebola victim to the local authority crematorium across town. Apparently the hospital crematorium's furnace was being connected to a new gas supply and would be out of commission for three days.

Valtmeier was prepared. His long experience in the Stasi years before had taught him the many ways in which people could be caused to disappear, or have their identities altered in the records. Ah, yes, those records – banks and banks of grey filing cabinets under lock and key in grey vaults and warehouses in grey concrete office blocks, supervised by anonymous grey men in their black suits and suspicious black minds, endlessly filling sheets of cheap paper with typescript biographies of the foibles and weaknesses of every comrade citizen in utopian East Germany.

Substituting a bagged corpse with another body in an identical bag, and switching the labels and documents accompanying each, was mere child's play to Willi Valtmeier. He had simply persuaded his new young colleague to leave the transportation across town to him and to go and read the paper in the hospital canteen instead. After all, a sealed corpse hardly needs the attendance of a paramedic.

CHAPTER
FOURTEEN

B UT WILLI VALTMEIER WAS FEELING VERY FRUSTRATED. He had set up the perfect body heist. All had gone to plan. Handed over to another of Stetten's accomplices on the outskirts of Geneva, the corpse had gone west in its butcher's refrigerated van to the Spanish coast.

And then that damned Spanish trawler crew had spectacularly ploughed the entire manoeuvre and blown the thing sky-high, to the extent that the mysterious body in a bag had featured in press reports throughout Britain.

To cap it all, Stetten had immediately expected Valtmeier to produce another corpse! It could be months before a similar opportunity arose, and probably even then it would require yet another infiltration in another city, and in yet one more carefully crafted disguise.

He had had enough.

*

Stetten began to feel the pricking of sweat down his spine beneath his Turnbull & Asser shirt, as he continued to sit immobile at his embassy desk, staring unfocused out across Holland Park in the pale sunshine.

Only a week away from the end of May, and his so-called colleagues (in reality, his masters) had to have a viable viral source in their Bristol laboratory at least by the 20th July. Time was running short. Very short.

Valtmeier was good – exceptionally good. Stetten had used other finders in the past on a variety of projects, but Willi was tops. He could not afford to lose him now.

He had always adopted 'divide and rule' as a working principle in his dealings with his underworld agents. Bitter experience had taught him that it was safest for each of them to know nothing of the others.

Coke and Jacko worked together, of course, but Jacko was merely a labourer. Coke was loyal. He had to be, as Stetten had a watertight hold on him which, if passed to the Metropolitan Police, would undoubtedly put Coke in prison for a very long time indeed. As they happened now to be in the same city, maybe Stetten could get Coke to talk to Valtmeier and persuade him to keep going.

After all, the Tomlyn debacle could work to their advantage in that respect. If Tomlyn had put two and two together and succeeded in briefing the British authorities, Valtmeier's own cover could be quickly blown and Interpol would be on his heels within a matter of days. Coke's task of constraining the Tomlyns for a couple of months would ensure Valtmeier's continued freedom to use his initiative and complete his own role. Coke had a hold on him.

Besides, the two hundred thousand pounds Willi Valtmeier was to receive in US dollars on the successful delivery of a viral source to Avonmouth was a material consideration.

Stetten lifted the phone and punched in Coke's mobile number. "Coke? Stetten here. Look, I want you to make contact straight away with someone working for me in Lausanne – Willi Valtmeier. He's a driver for a private ambulance company attached to the University Hospital. I'll give you his number.

"Now listen. He's on the same project as you are, but you don't need to know his role. What you do need to do is explain your job of tailing the Tomlyns and preventing them from blabbing to the authorities about that corpse. Lay it on thick that Valtmeier's own cover will be blown sky-high if the British get wind of the Lausanne connection and," here Coke could almost feel Stetten thumping his fist on his desk down the phone, "he's just got to produce the goods as a matter of utmost urgency. Otherwise we are all going to be knee-deep in the slurry. Got it?"

"Got it, chief. Knee-deep in the slurry. I'll get Jacko to keep an eye on the Cornish duo while I meet up with this Willi bloke tomorrer mornin' if I can. By the way, I'm runnin' out of funds, boss. Can yer transfer another five hundred or so?"

A few minutes later, Stetten had ended the call and sat chewing his nails, dreading his next task. There was no alternative – he had to call a meeting of his own clients (or colleagues, or compatriots, or whatever euphemism he cared to use) and bring them up to date on the progress of the project, or abject lack of it. It was not going to be a pleasant occasion. These meetings were not improved by the fact that half the foregathered spoke no English, and the other half were under the erroneous impression that they did. When the conversation became really heated, communication tended to revert to a variety of dialects based on the Russian alphabet. Fortunately, Stetten could understand several of those languages – but often on those occasions wished he did not.

*

DCI Drury patted his jacket pockets. Airline tickets, passport, Devon and Cornwall Constabulary passbook, Swiss gendarmerie contact confirmation and Interpol acknowledgement. Tin of peppermints.

Alongside him in the Heathrow waiting area sat young Detective Constable John Boyns, flushed in the face and trying not to look too excited. This was an adventure indeed. He had made a good impression on his senior officer ever since his first inspired suggestion to circulate the corpse's photograph around European hospitals.

"Right, lad," said Mike Drury, "while I have a nice doze on the plane, I want you to jot down carefully your plan as to how we pursue these inquiries. First, we are due to meet the clinical director of the hospital in Lausanne; we have an appointment with him already set up for tomorrow morning. Make a list of the questions we want to ask him. You've got the photographs of the body?"

Boyns nodded.

"OK. Remember, whoever is behind this heist will know it has failed and will presumably be trying again. Though not necessarily in Lausanne, of course."

Their flight was called, and the two officers joined the boarding queue for Geneva. Lausanne was shortly to become a little crowded with Cornish and Cockneys with a shared focus, and a German whose focus had become distinctly fuzzy.

In the meantime, the clock was ticking for all concerned – and for many, perhaps thousands, entirely unawares.

CHAPTER
FIFTEEN

I T WAS JUST A COINCIDENCE THAT, ON THE FOLLOWING morning, four men happened to enter the imposing entrance hall of the Centre Hospitalier Universitaire Vaudois in Lausanne at the same moment.

Willi Valtmeier and Coke were a few seconds ahead of DCI Drury and DC Boyns – indeed, Willi in his driver's uniform held the door open for the two men behind him. He quickly ushered Coke into a corridor leading to a quiet spot by a storeroom, while the police officers waited to be taken up to the clinical director's office on the first floor.

*

The director had done his homework in anticipation of his interview by the British police. He had prepared a list of all the personnel, including those at the local authority crematorium, who had been involved in the transport and cremation of the unfortunate patient who had, despite the hospital's best endeavours, died of his severe Ebola infection back in March. The local council and the private medical transport firm had been most obliging and cooperative. They were confident that all their procedures at the time had been entirely in order.

Drury scanned the list. The local staff from the council crematorium at the Centre Funéraire de Montoie largely and unsurprisingly possessed names of French extraction. There were six employees of the private ambulance contractor who worked regularly at Lausanne hospital. Working for a German firm drawing staff mainly from German-speaking cantons for its Swiss contracts, their names were mainly of predictable origin – Dolmann, Endorfer, Landemann, Valtmeier and so on. These last two were the paramedic and driver respectively on the day in question.

Armed with the details, Drury and Boyns took themselves off to the gendarmerie to set about the process for police interviews of the council's and contractor's employees concerned.

*

Meanwhile, Coke had thoroughly put the wind up Willi Valtmeier, who offered to assist him and Jacko in seizing the Cornish couple and securing them as a matter of urgency. He had to find a new identity and another body-snatching opportunity well away from Switzerland, but recognised that he had to protect his own back immediately, preferably that very day. Who knew how close those Cornish busybodies were to contacting the Bodmin police with their suspicions?

He and Coke left the hospital by a back entrance and rejoined Jacko at the little B&B over the corner cafe down in the town. There Willi shed his driver's uniform and donned civilian clothes he had stopped to purchase on their way down in the Citroën van. The uniform he stuffed into the cafe wheelie bin out on the pavement. His employer had seen the last of Willi Valtmeier.

The three of them then crammed into the van and drove fast along the shore road eastwards, back to Vevey.

Now to find those Cornish innocents. They should be easy game for a former Stasi officer, Valtmeier thought to himself.

*

Jill and Petroc Tomlyn had been intrigued that morning to come across a large restaurant on the Vevey shoreline devoted in its name and decor to Charlie Chaplin. Its walls were covered with black-and-white photographs of the great comic actor, and he was 'themed' everywhere, including the menu.

According to their waitress, Chaplin and his wife had lived out the last years of their lives in the village of Corsier on the north-western edge of the town, Chaplin having been declared *persona non grata* in the USA for his leftist political views. He had been popular locally, and was buried with his wife in the cemetery in Corsier.

After lunch the Tomlyns walked up the hill out of Vevey, through the commercial district, and soon found themselves in what was still a distinctive, pretty village square; on one side a handsome stone church, recently restored, and on the other an attractive old inn dating from the 1300s, the Hotel de la Place, its outside dining area and steps overhung with the most photogenic wisteria.

It was a glorious sunny day and the couple had largely put to the back of their minds the curious encounter they had made the previous day with the two officers of the Metropolitan Police. This was a day for holidaymaking, and they were determined to make the most of it.

They strolled down the narrow Chemin de Meruz to inspect Chaplin's uncharacteristically dignified stone table-tomb (and were surprised to see that his fellow actor James Mason was also commemorated in that tiny graveyard.) At the bottom of the hill they spotted on the other side of the main road the booking office and entrance to the *funiculaire* cog-wheel railway line that ran, almost straight as a die, up the side of Mont Pèlerin towering above the town. On the spur of the moment they decided to take the *funiculaire* and walk through the woods at the top of the little mountain, which according to their tourist map had several well-marked footpaths. Just the day for it.

As they crossed the busy road, a small grey Citroën van careered around the bend behind them and suddenly, for no apparent reason, pulled over onto the pavement. One of its occupants was pointing excitedly and speaking to his colleagues in a most animated fashion. The driver reversed into a small side road and parked none too neatly behind a Nestlé van. All three men tumbled out of the vehicle and ran to the corner, scanning the open ground up ahead.

Not having eyes in the back of their heads, Petroc and Jill noticed none of this. They bought their tickets and waited on the little platform for the cog-wheel train to make its way slowly down the hill to its buffers. The doors opened and they stepped on board.

They were not alone. A noisy group of schoolchildren, several women with their shopping, and a particularly loud and voluble family of American visitors all crammed into the single carriage around them.

Designed to run upright along a forty-five-degree slope, the carriage seating was multi-tiered like a tiny theatre auditorium. The Tomlyns were swept by the crowd down to the lowest level with a panoramic view of the buffers, but shortly to prove to be the best seats of all for watching the vista of town, lake and mountains opening out below them as the train made its sedate way up the side of Mont Pèlerin.

Facing downhill, and well below the carriage doorway, they naturally failed to notice the rather breathless entrance of three slightly cagey gentlemen just as the train doors were about to close. For some reason these men chose to face uphill, thereby missing altogether the stunning landscape unveiling itself behind their determined backs.

The train gradually emptied as it slid to a halt at three or four stops on the way up. By the time it reached its upper terminus, the Tomlyns and the Americans were virtually alone – except, that is, for an unsmiling, obviously Germanic character with a bristle hairstyle, and two colleagues behind him who appeared to have dozed off under their hats.

Petroc and Jill strode off up the road towards the deep woodland of fir and birch.

CHAPTER
SIXTEEN

THEIR MAP SHOWED THE ROUTES OF SEVERAL MARKED
footpaths. They chose to strike off the tarmac road after a mile
or so, and took a narrow lane to the right, which would lead them
to a woodland footpath running north-west along the spine of
Pèlerin to its densely treed peak, and then rejoining the main road
outside a vast and complex steel structure that housed a variety
of radio masts and other kinds of transmitters and receivers for
national communications.

They reached the footpath and were relieved to see that it was
clear and well signed. The little yellow markers nailed to trees along
the route indicated this to be a cross-country skiing path during
the winter.

The day was moving on, and the Tomlyns were anxious to
keep up a good pace in order to complete their circuitous route
back to the *funiculaire* terminus that was now far below them away
to the south. They were not keen on the prospect of negotiating

these dark paths and lanes, overhung with thick fir trees, in the dusk of an evening that already threatened low cloud and rain later.

After half an hour's steady hike along a most attractive track, with occasional views to the north revealing green valley pastures (many with their archetypal Swiss timber huts for winter shelter and hay for the cattle), they came out into a beautiful clearing of short grass carpeted with tiny yellow-and-white narcissi just in bloom, where they paused for breath.

Before them stood a large, imposing building in heavy brown-creosoted timber, under a pale green corrugated-iron roof that extended all around in an elegant overhang. A sign on the gable end identified it as a chalet, built in 1819. Along the far side, the roof extended out over a large, open sitting-out area furnished with about a dozen sturdy wooden picnic tables and benches.

The place was entirely deserted. Heavy plank shutters were tightly closed across the windows, and the stout doors firmly locked and barred. This was evidently a cafe and resting place for skiers in the winter, and perhaps also open for the high-summer hiking season that would commence in a couple of months' time. Then it would be transformed into a lively and colourful centre of refreshment for visitors, loud with conversation and occasional music. Now, the building was silent – dark, bleak and formidable, its bulk looming out of the lengthening woodland shadows of early evening.

Jill shivered a little as they gazed at it, and glanced up at Petroc for reassurance before resolutely stepping off again onto the path.

Petroc followed, and as he did so noticed a movement in the trees behind them. A brief adjustment in shadow was all it amounted to, although it was accompanied by the snap of a dry stick underfoot somewhere back there in the gloom.

He hesitated, waiting to see whether another walker or two would emerge to join them on the path, but there was nothing. He shrugged, and resumed his way behind Jill as they left the open clearing and once more entered the forest beneath the thick canopy of needled branches that was rapidly shutting out the remains of the pale sunshine overhead.

The track soon narrowed to a path up a muddy slope for a dozen yards, and they had to concentrate on the rough ground to avoid losing their footing.

Suddenly from the left, out of the bramble and low brush alongside the pathway, there came a flurry of movement and breaking twigs, and something large and heavy careered into Petroc's shoulder, sending him sprawling to the ground, his face landing in the soft, deep mud.

Then he heard a muffled yelp from Jill up ahead, before a scratchy hessian sack was thrust over his head and his wrists were painfully bound behind his back with what felt like sticky parcel tape.

He went to yell out in anger and fear, but instead received a mouthful of sacking as more parcel tape was wrapped several times around his head across his jaw, forcing his mouth open.

A voice in English, with a strong German accent, spoke close to his ear in tones that brooked no argument. "Nice and quiet, Mr Cornish Man. Do not struggle and you vill not get hurt. You and your goot lady will come with us a short way along the path. I vill hold your arms and guide you. Come."

And Petroc felt strong hands grip his upper arms and lead him slowly, stumbling back down the slope the way they had come.

Soon they were walking on grass, and then they came to a halt. From right in front of Petroc came the unmistakable sounds of a door latch being jemmied open and rusty hinges creaking. He was pushed forward over a threshold (on which he nearly tripped), and into an enclosed space that, even through the hessian sack, he knew to be very dark.

"Sit down," ordered the German. "Zare is a bench behind you. I vill remove the bag from your head and you vill make no

79

noise – othervise it will be the worst for you. *Verstehen Sie* – you understandt?"

Petroc nodded and sat down. Jill had clearly been given a similar instruction outside by another person, as he heard her stumble in and felt the bench move as she sat back next to him against the wall behind them.

"Don't move your heads, or you might be hurt," the German warned as he cut the tapes around their mouths with what was soon to be revealed as the particularly sharp, pointed blade of a hunting knife.

At once, both Tomlyns could see in the gloom the figure of the brush-headed German standing over them, still brandishing his knife.

Then, through the doorway, black silhouettes against the fading light outside, two other figures entered; the voice of one of them immediately recognised by both of their bound victims.

"So, we meet again, my nosy friends," sneered Coke with a smile. "Welcome to the safekeepin' of the Metropolitan Police!"

A duet of sarcastic sniggering followed this greeting, from the speaker and the man behind him, both now acknowledged by Petroc, with a sinking heart, as the two 'police officers' who had interviewed him all those weeks ago in the Coastwatch station on Cape Cornwall. He looked round at Jill and saw in her eyes the message *I thought as much, didn't I?* Petroc dropped his head and stared at the rough timber floor. From the very outset of this affair he had been hoodwinked, duped. Goodness only knew what ramifications this had, not just for him and his wife, but for countless others if their conspiracy theory was now to prove all too accurate.

Coke had a torch, and had moved off through the building to see what lay within. Above the large interior dining area, locked cloakrooms and a kitchen with its storerooms (empty out of season) was an upper floor gained from a steep wooden staircase and divided into four rooms; presumably bedrooms when the chalet was first occupied as a family home. They were largely vacant, but held a variety of seasonal items such as bench cushions, boxes of menu cards, and a quantity of colourful bunting.

Just the job, for the time being.

SEVENTEEN

THE SAME EVENING, DCI DRURY AND DC BOYNS, accompanied by a sergeant from the Swiss gendarmerie, were sipping coffee and awaiting the arrival of their first interviewee in the central Lausanne police station.

Georg Landemann had taken some tracking down. The local police had eventually found him in a bar way over in Montreux, where he was known to have a number of friends. Their search for the other possible suspect, Willi Valtmeier, had so far drawn a blank.

"*Monsewer Landemann*," began Drury, "*pert étra vous parlay l'Onglais?*"

"Yes, monsieur, by all means," Georg replied, to Mike Drury's relief.

The Swiss sergeant frowned. His own English was decidedly sketchy.

Drury took Landemann carefully through the events of the day back in early spring when he had been instructed, only a few days after starting his job as paramedic in Lausanne, to accompany a corpse for cremation in Montoie with his colleague, the driver Valtmeier.

Georg, a young man who had only been given this, his first job, with the ambulance contractor at Christmas, was clearly nervous and ill at ease.

He's hiding something, thought John Boyns. At a glance from his boss, he took over the questioning. "Mr Landemann. Think very carefully. You assisted your colleague in loading the stretcher with the bagged corpse into the back of the ambulance?"

Georg nodded.

"And then did the ambulance go directly to the crematorium without stopping anywhere? Did you help, or at any rate watch, as the corpse was unloaded and taken custody of by the crematorium staff on your arrival at Montoie?"

Silence.

"Well, Mr Landemann? We are waiting for an answer."

Georg lowered his head onto his arms, which were outstretched on the table that separated him from his interlocutors. Boyns' pulse quickened in anticipation of a revelation.

"Monsieur," Georg whispered, looking up at the Swiss policeman, "does my employer need to know what I am telling you, please? I am afraid for my job." This he repeated in French, as the Swiss was clearly struggling to follow the conversation.

The gendarme shrugged. "*Pas nécessaire.*"

Landemann then reluctantly confessed that he had acquiesced to Valtmeier's suggestion that he go back to the hospital canteen for a snack and leave the delivery of the corpse to the driver alone.

Boyns grimaced in disappointment. This was not the confession he had been hoping for. He looked across at his senior officer and raised an eyebrow. The real culprit was now all too evident.

Drury shook his head, and stood up. "In that case, Mr Landemann, it would seem that you can help us no further. Thank you for your co-operation. Please ensure that the gendarmerie here are informed of your whereabouts over the next few days, in case we need to ask you any more questions." He turned to go.

DC Boyns made to follow, but then hesitated and sat down again. "Mr Landemann," he said, "when did you last see your colleague Willi Valtmeier?"

Drury stopped at the door.

"Well, sir," answered Georg, "I saw him this morning, in fact. I was just going off shift and walking down the corridor from the ambulance bay. Willi was standing in the corridor chatting to a man I didn't know. I don't think he noticed me – he was looking very worried at what this man was telling him, that's for sure."

"And can you describe this other gentleman?" coaxed Boyns gently.

Georg Landemann thought for a moment. "He looked English to me; don't know why. Dark suit, a bit crumpled..." And he went on to give a very fair description of Coke, which was meaningless, of course, to his audience.

DC Boyns made a careful note.

As they left the police station a few minutes later, Drury gave his colleague a pat on the shoulder. "Nice work again, John, well done. I'm getting slow. This deserves a pint if we can find one. Then we must find Valtmeier. He's our man, no question about it. We'll talk to our gendarmerie friends first thing in the morning."

And they walked to the nearby taxi rank in the gathering darkness.

*

At about the same time that Drury and Boyns eventually found a bar to their liking and were sipping a disappointingly insipid pale lager and wishing it were a tawny bitter, events way up in the forest of Mont Pèlerin had settled down for the night.

The three kidnappers had agreed that Valtmeier should remain in the chalet to guard their captives at least until morning. This was familiar work as far as he was concerned, and it was abundantly clear to the Tomlyns that any attempt to create a noise or achieve escape would be met with professional violence.

Strong-arm stuff was not Coke's style at all, and while Jacko had the necessary nasty streak, this was not matched by physical strength. Neither of them was accustomed to spending a watchful, cold night in discomfort and without food or water. Willi Valtmeier, in contrast, was in his element, and relished it.

So Jacko and Coke had stumbled back under feeble torchlight through the woods and down the lanes and road as far as the imposing Hotel Mirador near the top of the *funiculaire*, where they found a taxi to return them to the little Citroën van they had left way below in Vevey. They returned to their B&B in Lausanne and walked into the town for a long-overdue supper to which both were determined to do justice. In the morning they were to load up the van with provisions and blankets and drive up the steep lanes onto Pèlerin as far as there was vehicular access, to rejoin Valtmeier at the chalet and decide what to do next.

They spotted a rather English-looking bar, and entered into its warmth rubbing their hands in anticipation of a large meal. The bar was crowded, but they found a small table to themselves and studied the rather basic laminated menu.

Having made his choice, Coke gazed around the room and reflected on the day's excitements. The premises were extensive; the bar itself the central hub of a circle of four or five partitioned dining areas openly facing it. Almost all the tables were occupied, under rather dim wall lighting, by a varied clientele – earnest professional men enjoying working dinners, young couples out for the evening, and middle-aged regulars reading their newspapers over long-drawn-out cups of rapidly cooling coffee or glasses of red wine.

The crowd at the bar was noisy. It consisted largely of a group of French tourists determined to express their contrary views on all available subjects at maximum volume.

Coke noticed at one end of the bar a couple of businessmen, or some such, in grey suits, trying to converse over the hubbub at their elbow, nursing large glasses of pallid yellow lager. They struck him as being somehow rather out of place. Probably Brits, he thought to himself.

CHAPTER
EIGHTEEN

JILL LAY QUIETLY IN THE DARKNESS. SHE AND PETROC had found in their bedroom prison a heap of musty old cotton tablecloths, and had wrapped several around themselves before lying down on a pile of bench cushions.

She was really quite comfortable, if she could succeed in ignoring her rumbling stomach. Her head was clear, and she felt perfectly calm. Plenty of time ahead during the night to think this whole strange business through rationally.

Their warder had ordered them not to talk, or even whisper, waving his vicious-looking knife at them to emphasise his instructions. He sat on an upturned box by the door with his arms folded, his ice-cold pale blue eyes scarcely blinking and very much wide awake.

Petroc, she realised without very much surprise, was already fast asleep beside her.

Why had they been kidnapped? Based on what she had read

in novels and occasionally in the news, kidnappers usually held someone for ransom. That presupposed that there were people or organisations particularly keen to secure their release. No one knew or cared that the Tomlyns were in Switzerland except for a few friends back home in St Just, so she could rule that one out.

No; the answer must be the obvious one. Being found in Vevey by those two phoney Met Police officers the other day was too much of a coincidence. Those men must have realised that she and Petroc were there because they had discovered at least part of the truth about the Cape Cornwall corpse – that it had come from the CHUV here in Lausanne.

So, if we know that, what else might we know? And, more importantly, what might we be about to report back to the real police in Cornwall? Did we see through their phoney Met disguise when we had that conversation near the paddle steamer's gangplank?

We just have to be kept incommunicado. That's why we're here. But for how long, and for what ultimate purpose? wondered Jill as she lay there in the dusty storeroom of the remote chalet, buried in old tablecloths and listening to the rising wind through the dense forest firs that enclosed them all around.

*

Down in the centre of Lausanne, under the bright lights, the nightlife was warming up. Many of the more expensive shops were still open, displaying their glittering goods through plate glass and encouraging potential shoppers onto the pavements and into the pedestrian squares.

Coke and Jacko were not interested. They were still working their way through the menu in the bar, beginning at last to feel quite replete. Neither of them were conversationalists. An occasional grunt of satisfaction through their latest mouthful represented the extent of their small talk.

The two suited Brits squashed into the corner of the bar itself were on their second pint, demolishing small platefuls of stuffed olives and crisp frites. Coke noticed that the younger of the two, who had been sitting on his stool and facing out into the dining area, kept glancing his way.

Then suddenly the man met Coke's eye. When that happens between strangers the normal social reaction is to look away again quickly. On this occasion the man held Coke's gaze for a fraction of a second too long.

Coke frowned and carefully adjusted his chair to turn his back on the bar area. *No thanks, mate, you're not my type*, he thought to himself.

In doing so, he missed seeing the man at the bar nudge his colleague with his elbow and mutter something into his ear, trying to make himself heard in confidence over the din of conversation from the French group nearby. The younger man then withdrew from his inner jacket pocket a piece of paper, and passed it to his friend, who perused it carefully and handed it back. Both of them rather too deliberately stuck their elbows on the bar top and buried their faces in their lager glasses.

A quarter of an hour later, and Coke and Jacko had eaten enough. With a deep belch on Jacko's part, they stood, scraping their chairs back on the linoleum floor, and struggled into their coats. They left the building and ambled a little unsteadily eastwards in the direction of Ouchy to their corner-cafe B&B.

Neither could be bothered to look behind them. Separated by perhaps thirty yards, they were being cautiously pursued by a British chief inspector of police and a detective constable anxious to keep track of the man who fitted rather well the description given to them earlier in the evening by Monsieur Landemann.

John Boyns just couldn't believe their luck. Of course, this could be a wild goose chase, tracking a fine, upstanding citizen of Lausanne. But it was worth a try.

The two pairs of colleagues shortly reached their destination. DC Boyns made a quick note of the details of a small Citroën van which one of the men they were following had unlocked to retrieve an item from the passenger seat. Both then entered the side door of the cafe and closed it behind them, but not before Jacko had called across to Coke, "Jer want yer briefcase upstairs, mate?", and Coke had replied, "Nah, that can stay in t'van, ta. 'Ere, lock the motor 'n' I'll 'ave the keys. Early start termorra."

Two nonplussed police officers stood stock-still in the dark shadow of the street corner opposite the cafe.

"Bloody hell, Chief," whispered DC Boyns, "they're Cockneys."

"If we've got the right man," mused Drury, "this could be the link with Cornwall that we're looking for – well, with England, at any rate. Time, I think, to borrow an unmarked car from our gendarmerie friends. Tomorrow morning we'll tail that little Citroën van and see where they take us. Could be interesting. OK, John, back to the police station now and we'll fix something up."

The two officers walked quickly back to the town centre to find a taxi. This was going to be a short night by the time they got back to their hotel.

CHAPTER
NINETEEN

JILL TOMLYN LAY AWAKE, THOUGHTS RACING THROUGH her head. Close by, she listened to the measured breathing of her husband, who was quite clearly in deep sleep.

She could just make out the time on her watch – twenty past three. It was pitch dark in the room, but a vertical chink of pale blue light dimly revealed the ill-fitting join between the two closed shutters of the window above her head.

She formed a picture in her mind of what lay beyond the window. An open space of short grass, surrounded on all sides by thick forest except for the tourist track running south-east. She contemplated the absurd possibility of escape. If she could somehow get out of the building, perhaps she could get back to the road and down the hill to fetch help. Absurd, of course, with the piercing blue eyes of their captor watching for every false move. And that knife.

Then, after ten more minutes had passed, Jill noticed two points of interest.

Firstly, that vertical line of light between the shutters ran from top to bottom without a break. Surely if they had been secured, the thick metal bar latched across their centre would have divided the shaft of light in two?

Secondly, and this was where the pulse in her neck began to throb intensely, she realised she could quite plainly hear not one rhythm of heavy breathing, but two. Their warder had evidently succumbed as well.

Very slowly, she raised herself on an elbow and reached up with an arm to the window above her head. Inch by inch, and pausing with breath held between each movement, she explored with her fingers. To her surprise, there was no glass in the closed casement frame. At least, in the lower part there remained only the shards of broken glazing around the perimeter of the frame, held in place by the old putty.

Jill silently stood up, careful to let her tablecloth bedclothes fall without a sound. She tentatively patted the lower edge of the window frame, regretting this instantly with a suppressed inhalation and putting her hand to her mouth to lick the spurt of blood where the razor edge of a glass remnant had punctured her palm. Wincing, she gently eased open the shutters and looked out. In the glimmer of blue-green light she made out, beneath the windowsill, the shallow slope of iron roof that covered the outdoor dining area.

On an impulse, her resolution took hold. She gathered an armful of tablecloth and laid it as a pad over the jagged edge of the window frame. With a quick, frightened glance across the room towards the dim form of her captor slumped by the door, she put a knee on the sill and hauled herself up and over the opening, turned around and lowered both feet onto the sloping corrugations of iron roof at its junction with the wall some three feet below the window.

One shoe slipped on the mossy surface and she fell flat onto the roof, limbs splayed and fingers grappling for a hold. Her hands managed to catch the edge of the lead flashing at the peak of the roof pitch. She held her breath and waited, expecting any moment to hear a bellow of anger and see the face of the German appear at the windowsill, one hand brandishing that knife. But... nothing. Only the wind in the fir trees and a light patter of dried moss bouncing down the slope of the roof beneath her.

Her face screwed up in anxious anticipation, Jill let go of the flashing. Very slowly at first, then gathering pace, she began to slide down the slope of the roof. She tried to control the speed with the toes of her shoes, but with little effect.

Suddenly, her feet met an obstruction and she came to an abrupt halt. She opened her eyes and looked down. She had come to rest against the mesh upstand of a snow guard fixed to the eaves fascia board behind the gutter. A thudding sigh of relief escaped her as she realised that, at least for the moment, she was secure and unharmed.

Jill shifted her body sideways so that she was lying alongside the mesh and could look over the edge to the ground below. The grass was in deep shadow but she estimated that it lay about ten feet beneath the edge of the roof. Nothing for it but to ease herself over the low mesh fence, dangle her legs, and drop.

As she did so, her jacket lapel caught on the steel horn of a gutter bracket, which skewed her fall, causing her cheek to graze painfully down the sharp edge of the corrugated iron as she swept downwards. Her knees and ankles jarred severely as she hit the ground. Jill was unaccustomed to these kinds of antics, and did not think to let her knees bend to take the strain. She knelt on the turf on all fours, momentarily stunned. Lifting a hand to her left cheek, she could feel the wet blood and the sharp sting of the injury. Her jacket was ripped from collar to shoulder and the palms of her hands were raw from the rough slide down the roof. But she was in one piece.

After a few moments she got up, hopped about a bit, and then jogged south-eastwards to the road, stumbling occasionally but gradually getting her wind and pacing herself as fast as she could towards the dawn.

*

Despite Valtmeier's high opinion of himself as a hardened Stasi enforcement officer, in reality it had now been many years since he had put himself in extremis. He was out of practice and out of condition. It was not until almost five o'clock in the morning that he awoke with a start, feeling stiff and uncomfortable on his hard wooden box. The room was filling with daylight; a shaft of dust lit up across the floor, from a half-open pair of shutters on the other side of the room.

He glanced over at the heap of cushions and assortment of improvised bedding under which his two captives were almost completely hidden. One pile revealed the dishevelled head and shoulders of the Cornishman, his chest rhythmically rising and falling in slumber.

The other pile of bedclothes next to him revealed nothing. In fact, much of it seemed to be spread about, including two cushions right up on the windowsill.

Valtmeier leapt to his feet and crossed the floor in long strides, his right hand drawing his hunting knife instinctively from his belt.

The woman had vanished. Valtmeier swore long and hard in guttural Oder Valley dialect and stuck his head out of the open window. Below him was the unmistakable evidence of a body having slid down the mossy roof.

In vexation he slammed his fists down onto the window frame, instantly regretting this impulsive reaction as the jagged teeth of embedded window glass drove into his flesh. Willi Valtmeier was not a happy man. He roared in fury and kicked the sleeping form of Petroc Tomlyn lying at his feet.

Petroc awoke and jumped up in some confusion, momentarily having no idea where he was or what this vicious person was doing, rearing above him in evident anger. Then his situation flooded back into his befuddled brain. "What's going on?" he asked crossly. "Where's my wife, and what the blazes do you think you are doing?"

Valtmeier gazed at him balefully in silence for a long moment, sucking his right fist and rubbing his left down the side of his jersey. After a while he calmed down, and leant wearily against the wall. "Your wife, *mein freund*," he muttered, "has escaped." He jerked a thumb towards the open window. "While you were havink your sweet dreams, Mrs Cornish Lady climbed out and down zer roof. Well, I – how do you say in England? – take my hat off to her. A plucky woman, is your wife. Full of surprises."

Petroc turned to the window and stood there, looking out at the new day spreading across the forest, the snow-capped mountains away to the south in the hazy distance just beginning to catch the morning sun. *Good on you, girl*, he said silently to himself.

CHAPTER
TWENTY

A QUARTER TO SIX. COKE'S ALARM WENT OFF, AND HE levered himself off the bed, aching from head to foot. He had not slept well. All that frantic rushing about up in the woods, in his thin-soled lace-up shoes, had worn him out.

He sat on the edge of the bed and ran his fingers vigorously through his hair. *Too early yet to go shopping for provisions. The grocery shops won't be open for another couple of hours or so. A strong cup of tea is called for,* he thought to himself.

He unmuted his phone. Four missed calls, and a text message on the screen from Willi V. 'Fone me urgent,' sent at 5.15. He did so.

"That you, Coke?" came the instant response. "Listen, zer woman has escaped in the night. She'll be on to the gendarmes if she reaches a house. She's got no mobile with her – she left that behind.

"Look, I've got to get away. Stetten needs me for zer project – I cannot risk getting caught here. You and your mate had better get up here quick and cart zis Cornish man to hiding some other place. I've got to scarper, *mein freund*. You won't see me again. I'm off."

And Coke's phone went dead.

He rapidly pulled on his clothes, and charged across the landing into Jacko's room. "Gerrup, man. We gotta go pronto. The cops'll be on us up at the chalet if we're not bleedin' quick. The Tomlyn woman's escaped. Valtmeier's just phoned – he's doin' a bunk 'cause Stetten needs him fer sumfink else. Guess he's just gonna leave Tomlyn up there; then Tomlyn'll be phonin' the gendarmes."

Jacko tried to take all this in, while Coke paused for breath. He dragged on his shirt and trousers, picked up his boots and followed Coke down the stairs and out to the Citroën van. Coke revved the engine, and in a haze of blue exhaust smoke the van sped up the road, heading for Mont Pèlerin.

*

At five to six, a local smallholder from up in the hills above Chardonne ran into the reception hall at the Hotel Mirador on the escarpment above the town.

The night porter frowned at the line of muddy boot prints the farmer left behind him as he dashed across the pale flagstone floor to the desk, where he placed his huge, oily hands four-square on the polished surface, panting for breath.

"*M'selle*," he gasped to the young and astonished receptionist, "*vite, vite. Ici une Anglaise très malheureuse. Le gendarmerie, au téléphon, s'il vous plaît. Je ne parle pas anglais, pas comprends la problème.*" He turned around and beckoned to a bedraggled, unkempt figure, who had followed him into the hotel, limping badly.

Jill had lost one boot, and her thick hiking sock had completely worn through the sole. Her hair was full of twigs and moss, and one side of her face was dark and raw with congealed blood. She was gripping one wrist with the other hand, wincing at the pain from what must have been a severe sprain.

The girl on reception leapt up and dashed around the desk, taking Jill's elbow and guiding her gently to one of the deep, low, overstuffed armchairs in the entrance hall. Calling to the night porter to fetch a glass of water, she returned to the desk and stabbed the emergency number – 112 – into the telephone handset. After a brief conversation, she replaced the handset and walked over to Jill's chair, where she knelt down on the floor and took Jill's hand in hers. "The police are on their way, ma'am," she said in perfect English. "Just rest here till they arrive. Can I get you a cup of coffee?"

Jill nodded gratefully and murmured, "And please can you offer something to this kind gentleman who drove me down here from his farm? I expect the police will want a word with him before he goes home. He has been so helpful."

She closed her eyes and tried to relax.

*

At about half past six, DC John Boyns drove a borrowed Skoda estate into the street in which they had left Coke and Jacko the previous evening. His colleague DCI Mike Drury sat beside him, munching a large croissant filled with soft cheese. They turned a bend and parked alongside the curb opposite the corner-cafe B&B.

Drury stopped munching. "It's gone," he spluttered through a thick mouthful. "Damn and blast." The little Citroën van was nowhere to be seen.

They entered the cafe, which had just opened on their arrival with the clatter of the roller blind being released on the entrance door.

On enquiry of the proprietor, he went back into the domestic quarters and up the stairs to the guest rooms, returning with open palms and a shrug. "Both gentlemen have gone, messieurs, but will no doubt be back later. Their belongings are still in the rooms. Would messieurs care to wait, and perhaps have some *petit déjeuner*?"

Drury looked at his watch. Those two Cockneys could be anywhere. He thought for a moment. They had left full personal descriptions of the two men at the gendarmerie last night when they had made arrangements with their Swiss colleague to borrow the car. An alert had been issued instructing the Lausanne district officers to keep an eye out for the men and report their movements, but to make no contact. What more could Drury and Boyns do in the meantime? Valtmeier had not yet been found either.

He sat down resolutely at the cafe table and picked up a menu card. "Good idea, monsieur. Come on, John, I'm still starving."

Over breakfast, for which they were, at this early hour, the only customers, Drury tried to elicit from the proprietor all he knew of his two English B&B guests. Drury explained that he and his colleague were in the import/export business, had met the two Cockneys a few times and were considering employing them temporarily. He kept his story as vague as possible, largely because he knew precious little about importing or exporting, and hoped that this was likewise the case with the cafe owner.

However, his roundabout inquiries produced no useful information. The two gents had paid cash up front for a five-day stay, and the proprietor had scarcely spoken a word to them. In the guest book they had recorded their address as a guest house in Vevey; something the cafe owner had not actually noticed until Drury asked the question.

Then suddenly, Drury's mobile phone rang. It was a quarter past seven. He listened intently, a frown gathering slowly on his forehead but his eyes lighting up with increasing interest and concentration. "We're on our way, Inspecteur. We'll be right with you." And he hung up.

"The plot thickens, John. That was our Swiss gendarmerie inspector, phoning from a hotel halfway up the mountain at the back of Vevey. They were called to attend to an Englishwoman who had turned up at the hotel this morning with an extraordinary story. I rather think it might be our story. Come on, let's go. Get onto Googlemap. We are looking for the Hotel Mirador on Mont Pèlerin, east of here beyond Puidoux."

Boyns settled up with the cafe proprietor and they scrambled into the car.

CHAPTER
TWENTY-ONE

PETROC LOOKED GLUMLY OUT OF THE CHALET WINDOW, hands in pockets, and feeling cold and hungry. His German captor had confiscated his mobile phone, and had also found Jill's in the pile of cushions, pocketing that as well.

The man had then gone out onto the landing, shutting the bedroom door behind him. "Don't try anytink silly, my friend," he had sneered at Petroc; "I shall be close by. And keep very quiet, *verstehen Sie?*"

Petroc had heard him pacing the floorboards outside the room, speaking at length on his phone – initially in English and then another, longer call in German, but he could not distinguish the words. Then for twenty minutes or so, all he could hear was the man moving about in the corridor, the boards creaking under his step.

After a while, Petroc realised that all had been silent for quite some time. He put an ear to the door and listened intently for several minutes, but could hear nothing. He put his hand on the door handle, and hesitated. Dare he open the door and look out? He had visions of that sharp knife.

Come on, man, he said to himself eventually, *you're a Cornishman. Show a bit of courage.*

Ever so slowly, he turned the doorknob and inched open the heavy door, cautiously putting his head out through the opening and glancing quickly to left and right.

Nobody there.

He set his jaw resolutely, and trod carefully to the head of the stairs, looking down the stairwell. No sign of anyone. The front door of the chalet was askew, one hinge broken. He was just about to descend when a thought checked him. He returned to the bedroom and gathered up his coat and the two rucksacks and sticks that he and Jill had been carrying on their hike the previous day. Goodness, was that only yesterday afternoon? It seemed like a week ago.

He resumed his descent to ground level. The German might be outside, having a smoke, or relieving himself behind a tree. Petroc stood in the shadow of the open front door and cast an eye around the grass area and the fringe of trees facing him. No movement; nothing.

Maybe the German has done a bunk. Jill's escape must have unnerved him and he's run off. So Petroc began to convince himself. *Those other two characters may be back here any minute*, he realised with a frisson of alarm. *Now's my chance.*

He stumbled across the open space into the woods to the south of the chalet, and crouched behind a bramble thicket. Still nothing; not a shout or a movement, except for the fir branches rustling in the light morning breeze.

He glanced at his watch. Twenty-five past seven. He began to jog back along the path that he and Jill had so happily walked such a short time previously. A splash of colour met his eye ahead of him on the surface of the track. On reaching it he identified the shattered remains of two mobile phones which he ruefully recognised as Tomlyn property. He stopped to salvage the SIM cards. *Well, at least this supports the theory that the German has abandoned his role as prison warder*, Petroc thought with some relief. He managed to smile as he visualised the farcical scenario of his bumping into the back of the German as they both careered into the two Cockneys running on the same dark, narrow path in the oncoming direction. His smile faded as he began to appreciate that, sooner or later, he was almost bound to encounter the Cockneys before he could reach one of the farms and appeal for help.

He ran on, ready at any second to dart to one side into the undergrowth at the first sign of any movement ahead. After another half an hour, the clear blue light of cloudless sky, tinged with piercing rays of sunshine, filtered through the trees ahead and he knew he had reached the edge of the forest. He stopped in the shade of the last few firs, and caught his breath. Before him to the south lay the classic view of Switzerland, familiar from so many postcards and travel brochures. Under the hard blue sky and glaring sun lay the cattle pastures, with cows (and some donkeys) wearing traditional collar bells; the scene dotted with picturesque timber farmsteads and a whitewashed church. The glittering surface of Lac Léman formed a thin pencil line far below, and beyond that, away in the distance, a glimpse of snow-capped peaks faded into the haze.

Lumbering up the tarmac road, about a quarter of a mile away, was a small grey van. He was just about to step into the road and wave his arms to alert the driver with the intention of seeking help, and perhaps a lift to the nearest telephone, when his sixth sense alerted him and he hastily withdrew into the thicket and darkness of the trees from which he had emerged. Of course – he kicked himself – these could just as well be his enemies. He squatted down and kept very still.

The van reached the end of the metalled road, which petered out on the edge of the forest and continued in much-diminished form as a rough, muddy track into the trees. The driver tried to negotiate the van into the woods, but after a few yards its wheels began to spin in the soft, wet earth. It then reversed, with difficulty, back onto the grass verge alongside the road, and its two occupants jumped out and slammed the doors shut.

Petroc recognised them immediately, of course, and lay low. They were arguing loudly as they emerged from the van, and were clearly in a hurry. Still swearing at one another, they rushed off along the path into the forest to the west, one armed with a baulk of wood much like a baseball bat. They disappeared into the gloom and Petroc listened to their clumsy footfall, cracking twigs and slipping in mud, until the sounds faded to nothing, and he was once more alone.

Carefully, he crept from his hiding place and approached the grey van. An idea had just occurred to him that, for the second time that morning, made him smile. He tried the driver's door, which opened readily, and sat himself behind the wheel. No, the key was not in the ignition. *Damn.* He had never hot-wired a car's ignition system, and would not know how.

He looked around the interior for anything of interest, but it seemed bereft of any item that might afford a clue as to the purpose of the two Met impostors. He was just on the point of reopening the door, resigned to continuing his jog down the hillside, when his eye caught the gleam of the twin chrome chevrons of the Citroën marque on a small leather fob half buried in discarded sweet papers in the dashboard tray. With an air of triumph, Petroc extracted the object, on the end of which hung the ignition key which Coke had so hastily chucked into the tray a few moments before.

Thirty seconds later, Petroc was bombing down the road in the little van at impetuous speed. "I must find civilisation, someone who speaks English, and a telephone," he muttered aloud. "And above all, I must find Jill."

*

The two British police officers were ushered by a gendarme into the Lounge Piano Bar in the Hotel Mirador. There sat an Englishwoman being attended to by a nurse, who was carefully swabbing the woman's cheek. She had one foot up on a padded stool, clearly also receiving medical attention. Their colleague the Swiss police inspector was standing nearby, and came forward to greet Drury and Boyns.

They drew up chairs around the patient, and listened to the extraordinary story that Jill Tomlyn had to tell. She was still shaken and confused. Her narrative was a little hard to follow as she only began at the point at which the three kidnappers had ambushed her and her husband up in the woods.

After a few minutes, and a breather for Jill to take a cup of strong coffee, the door opened again and a man was ushered in by the receptionist. He too looked in a fairly sorry state; his face grimy, his hair matted, and his trousers spattered in mud. Drury frowned in concentration – this man was rather familiar; they had met before somewhere. Drury had a good memory for faces.

Petroc rushed across the room and knelt at Jill's side, wrapping an arm around her shoulders. "Jill," he mumbled hoarsely, "thank God you're safe. Are you OK? How on earth did you manage to get away?"

"I think, sir," interposed Drury, "it would be best to let your wife recover, and leave the questions till later."

Petroc looked round and noticed the British policeman properly for the first time. He nodded and turned back towards Jill – and then did a double take. Slowly he turned again and stared at the officer. "But... surely... aren't you Inspector Drury from Bodmin?" he faltered in bewilderment. "You're the man who interviewed me after I found the corpse at Cape Cornwall, back in March. Are you... I mean... is that what you're investigating over here?"

"I thought your face was familiar, sir," replied Mike Drury. "And yes, that is indeed why my colleague and I are here."

"In that case," said Petroc wearily, "Jill and I have quite a lot to tell you." He slumped down into an armchair and held his head in his hands. "Thank God you're here."

CHAPTER
TWENTY-TWO

COKE AND JACKO WERE NOT HAPPY. THEY HAD arrived, breathless, at the wooden chalet in the forest, expecting to find an angry Cornishman tied up or locked in the bedroom upstairs, secured by their German colleague before he had fled.

But the chalet was deserted. They had seen and heard no one. It was much too early in the day for ramblers.

They sat at a picnic table under the veranda roof in glum silence. Eventually, Jacko, who had opened his mouth several times to say something but had thought better of it, could be quiet no longer. "Ol' man Stetten inn't goin' ter be 'appy, mate. Us've garn an' lost both Tomlyns, 'n' that Valtmeier've scarpered, leavin' us right up Crap Street."

Coke glowered at his assistant. "I had worked that out for meself, y'know. If yer can't think of somethin' more constructive to say, then just keep yer trap shut."

They sat there wordlessly for a considerable time, feeling increasingly cold, stiff and hungry. Then, by unspoken assent, they got up and trudged slowly back to the roadside where they had left the van. But the van, of course, was gone.

"They'll have tipped off the cops by now," Coke muttered. "We daren't walk back down the road. And our B&B may well be watched. Nothin' for it but to cross country and find a railway station, an' get the 'ell out of Switzerland."

They turned and headed back once more up the hill.

*

At about the same time, Willi Valtmeier reached the road to Granges on the far side of the mountain that would take him to the main railway line to Bern. He aimed to catch a train at Gare de Palézieux and keep going up into Germany.

If he was to resume his commission from Pietr Stetten to find human tissue infected with a deadly disease, he had as a matter of urgency to renew his former East German connections and pick up some useful threads back into a medical institution where he could try again. More pressing than that, however, was the need to adopt a new persona with new identity documents and back history. The Swiss police, he knew, would now be close on the heels of Willi Valtmeier the paramedic driver. Willi Valtmeier must cease to exist, and quickly.

Before long he managed to hitch a lift in a ready-mix concrete lorry, and by lunchtime he was on the station platform at Palézieux, glancing anxiously at his wristwatch, impatient to get away before a heavy gendarme hand should land on his shoulder from behind.

He fingered his hunting knife in its sheath under his thick jersey.

*

In the meantime, back on the south slopes of Pèlerin, the Tomlyns had related their story to the British and Swiss police officers in the elegant Piano Bar of the Hotel Mirador, and were enjoying an overdue and much appreciated breakfast served with the compliments of the management.

The officers had retired to a small room behind the manager's suite. The Swiss gendarme inspector had now been joined by his superintendent. A brief session with the inspector's team was arranged for 11am that morning. Descriptions of the three kidnappers had been issued to all Swiss gendarmeries and to the police on the border crossings into Italy, France and Germany. Principal railway stations and all airports would be watched.

There was a sensitivity to the fact that the British authorities were involved, and that there may be an international conspiracy behind this kidnapping which might have tragic consequences as well as top-level political intrigue. At all costs, the matter must be kept from the press. Public panic was the last thing the authorities needed.

Government ministers in London were to be briefed the following morning, by the assistant chief constable of the Devon and Cornwall Constabulary, on DCI Drury's confidential email briefing from Lausanne. He would write that after lunch. He had been impressed with Petroc Tomlyn's take on the situation, and the conspiracy theory that Petroc and Jill had suggested as being behind the body theft.

The criminal operation had been sophisticated and expensive. This was more than some small-time crooked venture by a German van driver and two not overly intelligent Londoners. There had to be brains and money at the back of this – and at a high level. The corpse had clearly been lost at sea. Where was it being taken? From Lausanne it had been transported an inevitably long distance overland to the Atlantic, Mediterranean or English Channel, and from there by boat. Had the boat been going eastwards or westwards when it lost its cargo? Either way, the fact that the corpse had been put on a boat (with a refrigerated hold) at all could only mean that it was bound for Britain – or possibly a country further away, such as America.

America was, Drury reflected, unlikely. Logically the corpse would have been taken on board on the coast of Spain, Portugal or maybe the South of France, and then straight across Biscay and out into the Atlantic. In that event, it could hardly have been washed up at Cape Cornwall only a few hours after going overboard. No – it had to be Britain.

"We'll hang around here for another couple of days," Drury said to John Boyns later that afternoon, "in case the Swiss manage to secure any of the kidnappers. Then we had better get on home. The focus of this case will be back in England, I suspect. And in any case," he added, "I'm dying for a decent pint and a proper Warrens steak pasty or three."

DC Boyns had been studying a Lausanne-to-Bern 1:100,000 scale map that had been in the lounge bar bookcase. "You know, Chief," he mused, "I reckon our Cockneys and the German would be mad to try and make it back south to any town along the north shore of Lac Léman. From up there on Pèlerin they will surely have headed north. It is all open countryside, and they could avoid people well enough until they made it to the mainline rail connection, either to Bern or round the top of Lac de Neuchâtel west into France.

"According to the Tomlyns, the German will have had a couple of hours' head start, and is much fitter than the Londoners. He'll be well away by now, somewhere on a train. I reckon our best chance is to nab the Londoners while they're still on foot – probably somewhere within this arc," he pointed to the map, "between Puidoux to the west and Attalens to the east, with Granges at the peak."

Drury nodded, and took the map over to his Swiss colleague. A pincer movement was required from all three of these towns back towards Pèlerin.

The Swiss agreed, and issued the necessary instructions.

CHAPTER
TWENTY-THREE

WARM SUMMER RAIN FELL IN SHEETS ACROSS THE pavements of Holland Park in one of those sudden torrential downpours that take pedestrians by surprise at this time of year in London, or indeed anywhere else in Southern England.

Pietr Stetten held an umbrella aloft, but this had no mitigating effect on the water rebounding off the stone, saturating his trouser turn-ups and trickling into his black Church's shoes.

He was still fifty yards short of the embassy when his mobile phone began vibrating in his jacket pocket.

"Stetten," he barked into it, without breaking step. "Oh, it's you, Valtmeier. You're what? On the train to Bern? Well, I hope you and Coke have satisfactorily secured those Tomlyns. Have you got a new lead to follow yet for body tissue? This is getting urgent, you know. Try your old haunts east of Berlin; that's your best chance, I exp... sorry? You *what*?! Tomlyn's wife escaped – and probably Tomlyn too by now?" Stetten stopped instantly on the pavement, causing a woman close behind him to barge into his back with a clash of dripping umbrellas and soft expletives, before she passed him with a withering look which he barely noticed. He stepped into a secluded doorway. "So they've seen you, Coke and Jacko together as kidnappers." And of course, realised Stetten, recognised Coke and his sidekick as the 'Met officers' at Cape Cornwall. The whole carefully constructed scenario was crumbling before his unseeing gaze along the soggy vista of Holland Park. He glanced needlessly at his watch. *By now, at least one Tomlyn will have reached the Swiss police and given them their story, including the links back to events at Cape Cornwall. And,* he realised, *Coke and Jacko are now on the loose on Swiss soil, with or without Tomlyn in their clutches.*

"Valtmeier?" Stetten jolted himself back to his phone call. "Keep your head down and get the hell out of Switzerland, understand? I want you back on body parts."

Willi Valtmeier seized his opportunity. "Not so fast, *mein Herr*. Your English and Spanish friends screwed up my best success vith the Lausanne corpse. That vas zer perfect deal; I reckon I haf completed my side of zer contract. I want my money and out." He paused for negotiating effect.

Stetten remained speechless, frozen to the spot in anger and fear. His socks were now saturated, and he could feel the cold, clammy grip of waterlogged worsted around his ankles. The rain was, if anything, getting heavier.

"On zer other hand," resumed Valtmeier after a calculated interval, "I might be persuaded to try again. I haf another possible lead vith an old comrade of mine up in Potsdam. That vill require another seventy-five thousand pounds, on top of zer two hundred you already owe me. Do ve understand each other, *mein Herr*?"

With that, Willi Valtmeier pressed the red button on his phone and turned it to 'silent'. Let friend Stetten – how do you say it in English? – stew in his own juice.

He pulled down over his brow the woollen cap he had purchased, and settled more deeply into his train seat. Once through Bern, he should be safe enough. He had two additional fake passports in his pocket, in different names. Willi Valtmeier had never travelled anywhere in recent years without at least two passports.

*

Pietr Stetten closed the door of his private office on the first floor of the embassy. He dragged his heavy leather reclining chair over to the cast-iron radiator and turned the thermostat to maximum. Even in the early summer, the central heating in the building was still running and could be called on if required. After all, the State was paying the bill.

He removed his shoes and rested his feet and ankles on the heater. Steam began to rise from his trouser bottoms. It was not very comfortable.

He sighed and concentrated on his current predicament. His shadowy masters had given him a fixed budget for his role in the project. He had spent this already. Could he go back and persuade them to allocate another hundred thousand pounds to produce contaminated human tissue suitable for the project? The project would be dead in the water without it, of course. (Dead in the water – Stetten winced at the unfortunate irony of the phrase.) On the other hand, he tried to reflect objectively, what hope was there really that he could now achieve his task in time? Valtmeier was clearly becoming flaky, and he had nobody else to call on. Coke was, at that very moment, in serious danger of capture by the Swiss authorities, who would now have his description from Mrs Tomlyn. The Swiss would then contact the British authorities, and Coke would be interrogated.

Could Coke provide an identifiable connection to him; to Stetten? That was hard to answer. Stetten had, naturally, taken steps to prevent a direct trail. 'Pietr Stetten' was not the name by which he was known or employed at the embassy. His mobile phone, and the other cell phone on his desk, were very basic second-hand models incapable of being traced to their location. But Stetten had met Coke in person on more than one occasion. Coke could give a physical description.

And what about his masters? They would not hesitate to dump and expose Stetten if they themselves had to cover their tracks, or if he became a security risk. Or if he let them down.

After a few more minutes, warm feet and dry socks bred a new sense of hope, and he reached for his phone, pausing only to take a deep breath of determination. His co-conspirators could, frankly, like it or lump it. It was up to them.

His call was acknowledged, as usual, without identifying the speaker.

"Yes," said Stetten. "Listen – the delivery of material depends now on one man, if we have any chance of meeting the deadline. He's going cool on us following the loss of his last delivery, but I can bring him round. He has a new source. I shall need another hundred thousand pounds deposited—"

Here Stetten broke off, holding the phone away from his ear as the torrent of invective nearly ruptured the earpiece.

"—deposited immediately. I must get back to him this afternoon."

Now it was his turn to listen. "See here, Stetten," a guttural voice growled at him over the airwaves, "we are running out of patience. You need to understand your position well and good. If this goes belly-up through your inefficiency, our mutual friends are going to make your life very uncomfortable. Get me?

"Now, I will speak to them straight away and obtain a decision on the funds. I realise that we have little alternative, but I just hope for your sake, Stetten, that you are not trying to double-cross us on the money. I do not fancy your chances if that is your little game. I'll get back to you in an hour."

The call was abruptly ended, and Stetten subsided back into his chair with a long hiss of expended breath. So far, so good. He gazed dismally at the heap of paperwork piled up on his desk; all the accumulating business of his bona fide work at the embassy that was being neglected. He reached for the first document file and tried to concentrate. This would be another late night at the office if he was to avoid attracting unwelcome attention from his legitimate colleagues elsewhere in the building.

It was gone seven o'clock when his phone rang.

"Stetten, funds approved with some difficulty. Get your man on the job and deliver good material – now. No further excuses." And the line went dead.

Stetten reached under a stack of papers for his other private mobile. "Valtmeier?" he muttered. "Seventy-five K approved. Now get to Potsdam and deliver the goods. Where are you? In Zurich. OK. Don't let me down."

Pietr Stetten sat back and closed his eyes.

CHAPTER
TWENTY-FOUR

JACKO WAS EXHAUSTED. DARKNESS WAS FALLING rapidly, but he and Coke were still stumbling across country, north-west down the slope from Mont Pèlerin towards the railway line which they had spotted way below them in the valley.

Coke had been determined to avoid roads and inhabited terrain. He visualised the area crawling with gendarmes and dogs all intent on their capture. His imagination colourfully multiplied the number of officers actually employed in this task by a factor of at least ten, but nonetheless his ploy had been prudent, and so far they had seen no one.

Unfortunately, the woodland boundaries and the increasing number of grazing pastures they encountered on the lower slopes all had thorn hedges, thick bramble fringes, and stout wire fences. Constantly, he and Jacko had needed to detour or backtrack their intended route in order to make any forward progress at all. Their clothes were torn; their trousers and shoes thick with mud and grit. They had eaten nothing since supper the previous evening in the Lausanne bar.

Now there appeared a growing number of lights twinkling in the distance from a village – in fact, Puidoux, though they had no satnav app from which to identify it. Soon they struck a narrow road that presumably meandered eventually into the settlement.

Jacko slumped down onto the grass verge and held his head in his hands. "Listen, mate," he pleaded, "there'll be a pub or a caff down there. Fer Gawd's sake, I'm famished. I vote we 'ave a breather and find some nosh."

"What," responded Coke sarcastically, "all dressed up an' spruce like we are now? We walk into a caff like this," he gazed down at his lower limbs, "an' the manager'll be liftin' the phone to call the cops before we've even sat down."

"Well," said Jacko after a pause, "there's not much point in us catchin' a train an' pushin' across the border into France or whatever without a passport, is there?"

Coke stared at his colleague in silence for several long moments. "You don't mean to tell me," he enunciated very slowly, "you don't have yer bleedin' passport? How often have I reminded you to carry yer passport in yer pocket at all times, yer dozy blighter? Ye gods, Jacko, I'm lost fer bleedin' words."

Jacko looked up, chastened but defensive. "Well, you burst into my room this mornin' all of a lather, 'n' hauled me outta bed, yellin' at me ter get dressed an' into the motor. I didna have a chance to collect anythin'."

"So yer passport was sitting pretty on yer bedside table," sighed Coke, "all ready to be picked up by the fuzz. By now, they'll know all they need to know about you. I suppose it was yer own genuine one too, wasn't it?"

Jacko nodded numbly. "At least I've got me cash. Let's see if there's a food shop still open."

And so the two bedraggled erstwhile kidnappers limped into

Puidoux and found a brightly lit *boulangerie* that served snacks and hot drinks at a few metal tables at the far end of the shop. The teenage girl serving behind the counter scarcely gave them a glance. They sat at the corner table with their backs to the shop's customers and sipped hot chocolate in weary muteness. Three croissants each, with butter and cheese, followed in quick succession.

"Now what?" asked Jacko, sitting back in his shiny chrome chair and wiping his mouth with his sleeve.

"We get on a train, that's what," replied Coke. "We're just goin' ter 'ave to chance it at the border. If we get ter Zurich, we may find a way into Germany. Or, get Stetten to send a new fake passport – or two, under aliases, so we can both slip out under different names."

This idea pleased Coke, and he became a little more cheerful. "Look, there's a sign outside pointin' up the road to a station. Let's go."

*

Just north of the village was a small station platform, where the road came to an end. Coke and Jacko walked towards it with much more of a spring in their step, feeling reasonably replete from their slightly scrappy supper in the baker's shop.

The station lights and platform lamps lit the way. Dusk had now turned to darkness around them, and they needed to take care along the edge of the road, as several cars and taxis overtook them. A train heading north must be imminent, as the vehicles disgorged their passengers at the station entrance. A small bus passed them just as they were approaching the concourse.

They bought single tickets to Zurich at the little kiosk and strolled as inconspicuously as possible onto the platform, to stand in shadow away from the glare of the overhead lamps at the far end. The platform for the 'up' train was becoming quite busy. Smartly dressed commuters from Vevey offices were returning home alongside farmers' wives laden with their weekly shopping. Several children were being shouted at and herded away from the platform edge. An assistant stationmaster appeared with his torch, and consulted his watch.

Coke hated these moments. Waiting around anxiously, vulnerable and impotent, wishing that the train would speed up by force of his own concentration. Once aboard, in a crowd, with head down and affecting sleep, he would feel more confident of escape. As he had found on the road from Penzance through St Just to Cape Cornwall, he hated the open countryside, where every person was conspicuous. The anonymity of the large city was his comfortable habitat. There he could disappear, become invisible, go about his business with no one knowing or caring who he was or what he was doing.

Coke's musings were interrupted by the stirring of anticipation down the platform, and at last by the sight of the single headlamp of the approaching engine rounding the bend, growing in size and intensity as the train gradually drew into the station with a graunching of brakes. The carriage doors swung open, and a few passengers alighted. The prospective travellers began to converge at the open doors.

Coke nudged Jacko and they walked back down the platform to merge with the gathering groups and queues respectfully awaiting their turn to mount the carriage step. They hovered at the edge of the nearest group as two or three apparent stragglers hurried up behind them.

Coke and Jacko were next to mount the step when suddenly they both felt the firm grip of a hand on their shoulder; a grip that was not letting go. They twisted their heads around to look behind, and each met the steady gaze of a man whom they instantly knew from long experience to be a police officer. A third man stood back a pace, equally obviously a policeman, although all three were in plain clothes.

"*Pardon, messieurs,*" one of them said quietly but persuasively, "*un moment, s'il vous plaît. Nous voulons parler avec vous. Venez ici.*"

Coke's blood ran cold. He knew no French, but was in no doubt whatever as to the meaning of the words spoken – and indeed was under no illusion as to their implication for himself and Jacko in the foreseeable future. He glanced back at Jacko, who acknowledged him with a scowl and then turned again to his interlocutor. He knew when he was beaten. Coke nodded briefly and relaxed under the officer's hand.

They were led away. As they walked towards the police car outside the station, Coke's mobile began to ring in his pocket. He took it out and glanced at the caller's number. Stetten. He was about to return the phone to his pocket, but the gendarme guiding his elbow silently put out his hand, and, with a sigh, Coke placed the flashing phone into it.

"That you, Coke?"

Coke could hear the voice.

"Listen, you and Jacko must at all costs evade capture. Ideally, get home, but otherwise just hole up in a big city and I'll get you some passports... Coke? Are you there?"

The officer smiled faintly to himself, pressed the red button, and deposited the phone in his jacket pocket.

CHAPTER
TWENTY-FIVE

WALTHER MENSCH HAD BEEN A WELL-KNOWN investigative journalist in his time. Television viewers over the past twenty years had become accustomed to seeing his image, clad in flak jacket and green helmet, with a backdrop of live gunfire, reporting 'from the front' anywhere in the world; or attired in green overalls and a mask, holding the hand of a small child in the ruins of a Syrian hospital, interviewing a harassed and despairing medic who had run out of antibiotics and hope.

He now lay in an isolation ward of St Josefs-Krankenhaus hospital in Potsdam, clad these days in nothing but a patient's disposable gown and an oxygen mask. His bed lay within a sort of indoor tent that was kept tightly closed except for the comings and goings of well-masked and gloved nurses and doctors.

Somewhere on the other side of the world, during his investigations, he had picked up a bug known as the Nipah virus.

For too long he had been very far from adequate medical help, and now it was too late.

Walther was back in his home city now, not just because it appealed to him to complete the wide circle of his roaming life by returning to the place of his birth and childhood to die, but also because he had volunteered to offer himself, both alive and dead, to medical research into the appalling disease to which he was succumbing.

Of such are real heroes quietly made.

*

Willi Valtmeier (as we shall continue to know him, to avoid endless confusion) stepped off the train at Potsdam Hauptbahnhof.

He had grown his hair, now more like a bog brush than a nail brush, and had the beginnings of a pale grey beard.

He had an appointment with an old friend from his Stasi days.

It was, perhaps, an inevitable feature of modern unified German administration that many senior institutional posts were still held by competent individuals whose moral compass had once embraced the dark grey ethos of East German functionaries. Willi's friend Meinhard was one such. He held a lofty administrative position in the Federal Ministry of Health; a role from which he saw no reason to exclude other personal enterprises for his own enrichment. Why change the habits of a lifetime? He worked in the ministry's office in Berlin and lived in a fine house near the Botanical Garden of Potsdam, overlooking the Jungfernsee.

The following morning found Herr Meinhard in his garden at a wrought-iron table under a cream sunshade, sipping Peruvian coffee and listening to his old security-department colleague. Willi had lost no time in coming to the point. He needed a body. Or at least, a significant body part.

Meinhard waved him aside when he began to explain the purpose behind this curious request. The reason was of no interest to Meinhard. All he wished to discuss were the logistics and the price. As to the methodology, Willi, of course, had form and experience from his insinuation into the ambulance service in Lausanne. He outlined the process of his earlier success, but Meinhard shook his head.

"*Nein, nein, mein Freund,*" he interrupted. "*Nein.* This will not work here in the hospital system. We will think of something else."

Two weeks later, a plain white Mercedes refrigerated van pulled up in the yard of a specialist medical research laboratory in west Berlin; a building of no great architectural pretensions, but housing the most advanced expertise in the analysis of tropical diseases. The delivery that day comprised two insulated stainless-steel canisters packed in steel iceboxes; one from a Berlin hospital and the other from Potsdam. Both were trundled indoors, where the boxes were removed carefully by research assistants dressed in disposable overalls, masks and shoe covers, and whisked into the depths of a brightly lit lab, the airtight doors closing firmly behind them with a slight hiss and a click.

What happened during the early hours of the following morning was never fully established. At 3.30am a restless resident in a nearby block of flats, pacing his bedroom, unable to sleep, glanced out of the window through the slats of the blind, and noticed grey smoke rising lazily into the sky against the pale pink light of dawn creeping over the city from the east.

Very quickly, the smoke became blacker and rose more fiercely. By the time the insomniac citizen had telephoned the emergency services for the fire brigade and returned to the window, sparks were flying and tongues of flame licking through the eaves of the building two streets away below him.

By midday the fire was out. All that remained of the laboratory building was the blackened iron frame of the original structure, warped by the intense heat into a skeleton of curved joists and struts. Some of the equipment had been saved by the brave fire service personnel, but, on the warning given to them by the laboratory director, who had arrived on the scene at 4am, no attempt had been made to handle any container that might hold organic material. Small glass jars lay in pieces on the concrete floor, some of the glass molten and fused together.

The remains of two sizeable steel iceboxes were also found on the lab floor underneath the charred roof debris. In one of them (identified later as the property of a hospital in Berlin) was an intact insulated steel canister whose contents had been cooked to a crisp. Oddly, the other icebox was empty. It had been delivered the previous day from St Josefs-Krankenhaus hospital in Potsdam, but had not been opened.

The official inquiry into the fire some months later would note this fact, but, what with one thing and another, the Federal Ministry of Health would omit to pursue the question. The authorities at St Josefs-Krankenhaus would merely suppose that the mortal remains of Walther Mensch had perished in the unfortunate conflagration at the Berlin laboratory, and forget all about it.

Herr Meinhard would pocket a substantial sum of money via Willi Valtmeier in due course.

But now, the day after the Berlin fire, Willi had driven a Renault refrigerated van and a gleaming new icebox up north to the port of Bremerhaven, and met the skipper of a deep-sea trawler who was acting on instructions received from a source (unknown to him) in Holland Park, London.

The trawler was bound for Avonmouth, after a little fishing in the Western Approaches for the sake of appearances.

CHAPTER
TWENTY-SIX

THE HOTEL MIRADOR WAS NOW FREE OF SWISS AND British police officers and kidnap victims, much to the relief of the manager, whose valuable guests had been asking awkward questions over the past day or two.

The 'incident centre' had now returned to the main police station in Lausanne, where DCI Drury and his amiable Swiss colleague were drumming their heels, waiting for the political and diplomatic powers-that-be to stop bickering over who should have custody of the English kidnappers. The Swiss, understandably and with impeccable Swiss logic, were insisting that the very serious offence of kidnap was the reason for their present lawful arrest, and that the course of criminal justice should first be concluded in that regard. The British, perhaps with a more well-established overview of responsibilities on the international scene, were stressing the priority for intensive investigation of the conspiracy theory of mass public contamination for some political purpose. This was all best conducted in London, and the only alleged offenders so far in this scenario – the two Cockneys – should be returned to the UK, where they were, of course, British citizens.

This bureaucratic delay was not preventing Drury and Boyns from pursuing their interrogation of the two miscreants. Jacko was being particularly helpful, and had confessed his own junior role in the affair, starting with his engagement to accompany Coke to West Cornwall as a fake copper. Coke, in contrast, was sticking firmly to the 'no comment' response to questioning. His perspective was only a little wider than Jacko's, but he had the intelligence to believe that delay and obfuscation on his part could weight the scales in favour of extradition to Britain, and that, once there, the powers behind Mr Stetten might exert some influence in proceedings, to his benefit.

Jacko's revelations to the British police officers were of little value. He could only confess to the practical assistance he had provided in Cornwall and Switzerland on Coke's direct instructions. He genuinely knew nothing of the individual, or the purposes, behind the functions which he had been paid to carry out.

DCI Drury was feeling frustrated. This kidnapping business was, to him, an obstructive distraction from the far more important line of inquiry. Of course, kidnap was a serious offence and the Swiss were perfectly correct in treating it as such, but it was not why he and John Boyns were in Switzerland. They had much bigger fish to fry – or catch, at any rate.

What of this mysterious German, Willi Valtmeier? Name checks through Interpol had thrown up nothing. It was probably an invented alias; one of many employed by this individual. Now he had clearly got away. If he was still employed by his superiors, whoever they might be, he would presumably attempt another abstraction of dangerous human tissue, then to be transported to

Britain to some kind of laboratory where the lethal virus could be isolated and multiplied. If indeed that was the purpose – Drury agreed with Tomlyn's theory, but that was only guesswork. They had no evidence.

To obtain information on the purpose of this strange undertaking, he needed to find the next man above Valtmeier and Coke. Coke was not co-operating, and Valtmeier had slipped the net. It was all very tedious.

Drury's introspection was interrupted by DC John Boyns, who entered the office in Lausanne police station that they had been offered and drew up a chair.

"Been thinking, sir," Boyns began. "Our only possible trail at present is Valtmeier. He could have gone anywhere, but we can only go on the limited information we have.

"You'll remember his ambulance colleague, Landemann. He told us that, in conversation, Valtmeier mentioned that he had spent much of his life in former East Germany. Landemann mentioned that he recognised Valtmeier's accent as being from the Oder valley; Valtmeier then said that he was at heart a Potsdamer. Now, that's all we know. But we might as well try Potsdam as anywhere. He'll have jettisoned his name, obviously, and taken on a new identity. But we may pick up news of an odd missing corpse or some such, if we go up and sniff around.

"Also, sir, I've been thinking. It's not so far from the Berlin area up to the North Sea coast, which is only a hop to the coast of Britain. There aren't that many German ports. Our German colleagues would help."

Drury looked at his subordinate and then gave a wry grin. "My, John, you've been doing a lot of thinking. Good man."

He paused and stared out of the window for a protracted minute. "There's no point in us hanging around here, I agree. Let's leave the two Cockney jokers to the tender mercy of the Swiss, and go on the hunt. We could go north, south, east or west – but you're right, lad; we can only go on the evidence we possess, so let's head for Potsdam."

A day or two were needed for their superiors back home in London and Bodmin to arrange matters with the German police authorities and with Europol, and for Boyns to complete the paperwork in Lausanne. Then he and Drury took the train to Potsdam. There they briefed the *Polizeihauptkommissar* deputed to give them every assistance.

The British officers began by enquiring about any recent incident in which questions might have been raised about the disposal of cadavers or body parts from local hospitals. Here they drew a blank. The police had not been alerted about any such issue.

DC Boyns ventured a question. "Would it be possible, sir, to visit a local hospital in order to inspect the appearance of the types of container used in your country for transporting frozen human remains? I imagine that sometimes this material is moved from one location to another for analysis or research?"

"*Ja*, my friend," the German replied. "I expect that is so, and we can of course make such an arrangement." He lifted the phone and barked an instruction.

Within half an hour, Drury and Boyns, in the back seat of a police car, drew up outside the nearest hospital, St Josefs-Krankenhaus. There they were ushered courteously inside and down in the lift to the mortuary, to be greeted by a senior technician in pristine white overalls.

The large room, its walls and floor lined with gleaming ceramic tiles, was predictably immaculate; the resin table slabs and stainless steel shiny and sparkling. It was very chilly, and their breath hung in the air. At the far end was the entrance to the refrigerated rows of 'filing cabinets' where deceased persons could temporarily be stored.

A group of medics and technicians stood around one table slab, on which lay a naked corpse; that of a middle-aged man. His torso was partly cut open from rib to groin, and one medic was carefully removing something large, grey and wobbly.

John Boyns looked away quickly, beginning to taste the bile in his throat. The technician who was their host looked at him with amusement, and steered Boyns by the elbow to the other side of the room. Here on a shelf was a row of stainless-steel canisters of various sizes, mainly cylindrical and with quite complex steel-clip fastenings for their substantial lids. Drury and Boyns were handed rubber gloves and invited to handle two of the containers.

"Would these be standard items for use in all German hospitals?" Drury asked their host, who had been chosen for being a fluent English speaker.

"Certainly in most hospitals, *mein Herr*," was the reply, "and I have worked in several, including the Unfallkrankenhaus in Berlin. For any unusual laboratory work, for research or sometimes for forensics, we use these containers to transport material into Berlin, where until very recently – only last week – we had an arrangement with a private lab. But it burnt down, and we lost the sample and the canister in the fire. Very unfortunate."

Shortly after this conversation, Drury and Boyns left St Josefs and returned to their hotel. No leads so far, but (they reflected over dinner) that would have been a little unlikely.

CHAPTER
TWENTY-SEVEN

Petroc and Jill were on their way home to St Just. They had landed at Gatwick airport and were now heading for the train from Paddington to Penzance. They had undertaken to return to Lausanne as principal witnesses, and victims, of the kidnap on Mont Pèlerin if the matter should come to trial.

Jacko had pleaded guilty to the kidnapping charges; Coke was still prevaricating. However, Coke was beginning to realise that the British authorities had now more or less abandoned him and his colleague to the Swiss judicial system, and he was only playing for time.

If he pleaded guilty (which eventually he would), sentencing would take place without the need for live witnesses, and the Tomlyns were in fact never to be recalled to give evidence in court.

*

Meanwhile, Pietr Stetten was beginning to feel rather happier. At last, a secure sample of body tissue was again on the way to Avonmouth aboard a refrigerated fishing trawler. Valtmeier had come up trumps for the second time, and surprisingly quickly.

Stetten just hoped that this time, the passage of the vessel would be unimpeded, and that, a few days hence, the shiny steel cylinder would be ashore and on its way to his client's makeshift laboratory in Bristol. Once it was safely delivered there, Stetten's responsibility would end – provided that the Nipah virus in the tissue was alive and well, and capable of reproduction. If not, his job would start again from scratch; a scenario which he frankly could not face, and from which he determinedly averted his thoughts.

He sat there in his Holland Park office, nervously drumming his fingers on the leather desktop. He was feeling helpless. He ought to be in control at this crucial stage of the project. What if his courier from Avonmouth to Bristol messed things up? What if the trawler skipper became greedy and demanded extra payment before releasing his cargo?

Nothing for it, Stetten decided with a sudden, emphatic thump of his fists on the desk. *I must get to Avonmouth myself and supervise proceedings.*

Within the hour he had hastily packed a case in his flat and was on his way to Paddington station.

*

The concourses of large stations, like airport lounges, are curious social environments. Single-minded travellers, intent only on timetable and platform number, normally fail to appreciate how delightfully odd the passing interactions and fleeting relationships can be between strangers following their own line in parallel with others, but where on the concourse those lines cross and merge in complex point systems, as though replicating the tortuous pattern of the steel rails themselves that lie beyond the station.

It is only when passengers are finally seated in the carriage that speculation begins to intensify as to another person's particular track, its character and purpose. Casual gazing out through the grimy window can often afford an opportunity to study at leisure the reflection in the glass of the person opposite. One is never quite sure whether catching the eye of the reflected face means that he too is conscious of the contact. Then there is the battle of wills over knee space and where to plant one's feet. This can be an early determinant of personal nature.

It came as a shock to Petroc that afternoon, as he and Jill negotiated themselves carefully into their table seats next to one another in the crowded compartment, how accustomed they had become in France and Switzerland to the spacious comfort of quite ordinary train travel in those countries. Sitting there as the train idled at the platform in Paddington station, on a hot day with wholly inadequate air conditioning and ventilation in the static coach, was a rude re-introduction to British public transport.

Petroc loosened his collar and eased one leg slightly to the left to avoid another collision with the pinstripe trousering opposite. He smiled briefly in apology. The expression of the man facing him did not flicker as he stared stonily out of the window.

"All right, my love?" Petroc turned instead to Jill by his side. "A bit hot and cramped, isn't it? It will be better once we start to move. We'll get a little air movement then."

"I hope so," replied Jill, fanning herself with her paperback. "Gosh, this is a comedown after those marvellous, roomy Swiss trains, isn't it?"

Petroc nodded, and this time just caught the eye of the man opposite, who had glanced across to Jill when she made that remark; then instantly looked away again.

Subsequently, Petroc noticed once or twice that this neatly suited and rather worried-looking individual directed his gaze involuntarily across the table before he suddenly rose and left the train at Reading.

*

Pietr Stetten was irritated. The seats all having been pre-booked, he had been unable to secure a first-class ticket on the earliest train to the West Country from Paddington, and had needed to suffer the unaccustomed indignity of a cramped economy corner seat in a heavily overcrowded carriage. He was overheated, nervous and out of sorts. This decision to rush to Bristol had been impetuous, and contrary to his normal pattern of careful planning and ordered routine.

His commission was so nearly complete. What could possibly go wrong? Valtmeier had assured him on the phone that the fishing trawler's skipper had, through his contacts, been selected as competent and reliable – provided he was paid. It would be a simple matter, then, at Avonmouth, for the canister to be collected and taken the short distance into Bristol by refrigerated van.

But Stetten was nervous. He was also uncomfortable in his three-piece suit, and perspiring heavily.

The train set off with a lurch from the Paddington platform. For a minute or two he jostled slightly with the man in the opposite seat for leg space and somewhere to put his feet without twisting an ankle. *This really is quite insufferable*, he thought to himself. He immediately decided to get off at Reading and wait for the next train to Bristol, organising a first-class seat accordingly.

The couple opposite him at the carriage table were clearly man and wife. He had noticed them struggling on board with two very large suitcases and a couple of rucksacks. They had also tried to cram too many small bags and articles onto the overhead rack. They had clearly been away on holiday.

Suddenly, Stetten's attention was arrested by a comment from the woman to her husband about Swiss trains. *Switzerland!* Stetten winced inwardly, and rapidly looked away. This was ridiculous – not every couple travelling from Switzerland were going to be Cornish kidnap victims. *Do get a grip on yourself*, he thought, *and stop being so paranoid.*

As the train slowed into Reading station, he rose with relief and (to use that archaic railway expression) alighted onto the platform as soon as he could.

He could not help himself glancing back in through the window at the returning holiday couple. He caught the eye of the husband and hastily moved on.

CHAPTER
TWENTY-EIGHT

T HE FISHING VESSEL *ESSENSTERN* WAS BY NOW MAKING
its way slowly westwards through the English Channel. It was
heavy going; wind against tide into a strong south-westerly gale.

The skipper knew these waters well. He and his crew, some
of whom were profit-sharing partners of long standing, had fished
the north-eastern Atlantic and the North Sea for many years.
The Channel was to them simply a roadway between the two –
or rather, as the mate often joked (he had visited London), like
Piccadilly Circus in the rush hour.

Just about due south of Portland, the wind was dropping and
the sky beginning to clear; but the sea state was massive, the bow of
the trawler smacking into each wave valley with a shudder, jettisoning
the displaced white water high into the air and along the deck in a
boiling froth to drain through the scuppers as the boat reared up
once more over the peak of the next great swell, to slam into the next
valley and repeat the remorseless cycle, over and over again.

Towards the end of the afternoon, the engineer hauled himself up onto the bridge to consult the skipper. "Temperature's rising in the starboard engine, skip. Been watching it for a coupla hours now. Coolant pump maybe. Impeller's OK, I've checked that. I can't take much apart to investigate in these conditions. Reckon we'd best reduce power 'n' go steady for a bit – I'll keep a close eye on the dial."

"*Ja*, OK, Hans. I'll drop the starboard revs 'n' compensate on the rudder. I'm keen to get through this soon as we can. Keep me informed."

They ploughed on into the evening and the mate took over the watch for the first few hours of the night.

Shortly after three in the morning, the red warning light for water temperature began flashing on the bridge, and its alarm sounded.

"Starboard engine to idle," snapped the mate; "port engine slow ahead. Where's that *dumkopf* engineer?"

At that, the engineer's head appeared around the wheelhouse door. "Stop starboard engine, Karl. I'm gonna have to get to the bottom of this. Water flow seems OK, but the engine's fighting against something; maybe a seized prop-shaft bearing, I dunno till I can get at it with a spanner."

"Well, we can't bob around in this sea, Hans. We've got to keep under way. I'll carry on with port unit only – it will give you smoother conditions in the engine room too."

They continued to make very slow headway through the night. The wind had gone around to the north-west and picked up again to a steady Force 7. At about five o'clock the skipper had changed course to keep head to wind, and to find calmer conditions offshore of the English coast.

As daylight crept up behind them into a bright, sunny morning, visibility improved rapidly.

"I've checked everything down below, skip," reported Hans

the engineer. "Engine, bearings, oil pressure all OK. Something is fighting the revs."

At that moment one of the younger crewmen, who had been securing equipment aft, clattered up the gangway and yelled into the wheelhouse. "Hey, skipper – look astern, will ya? We're towing sumpfin."

The skipper went to the door and, shielding his eyes from the low eastern sun, followed the crewman's pointing arm. There, astern of them on the starboard side, ran a long wake of rough water and the occasional glimpse of something snaky and shiny, submerged just below the surface of the water. "Damn and blast," the skipper exclaimed as he ran out with crew members in pursuit. "I know what that is. We've caught up some steel cable round the prop shaft."

He and the mate stared over the transom rail at what lay below them. A tangle of thick polypropylene trawl net and its principal heavy steel cable rose and fell in the wake of the boat, running from deep below their feet on the stern deck out behind them for about twenty metres. How much more of it lay fully submerged beyond that was impossible to tell.

"All right," sighed the skipper, "it could have been worse. Steady as we go on port engine. Karl, back to the wheelhouse with me, please. We must decide where to make land and get this bloody thing off in harbour with divers. Damn nuisance."

The two of them plodded back up to the chart display screens. By now they were about twenty kilometres south-west of the Lizard. Due north was Mount's Bay, offering shelter and calm water under the offshore wind.

The mate looked up the facilities available for ship repairs and fishing vessel support in Newlyn and Penzance Harbours. "Plenty of expertise there," he noted with a long sigh of relief.

"Get on to them on the blower, then, Karl," instructed the skipper. "I'm going to get some breakfast."

*

At much the same time that the *Essenstern* changed course north towards Mount's Bay, the Great Western train from Paddington was rattling around the coast at Dawlish in Devon, in and out of the red-rock tunnels and sprayed with seawater on each exposure to the waves impacting the buttressed rail line along the foreshore of the Channel.

Petroc and Jill smiled at one another.

"A bit different from the promenade on Lac Léman," Jill remarked, involuntarily flinching as each deluge of spray smacked against the carriage window.

"I must say, I shall be glad to get home," replied Petroc. "I've had enough excitement to last me my lifetime. Back to sleepy old St Just, back to comfortable routine and a decent cup of tea. Can't wait."

But events were not to pan out quite so simply. Once again the far west end of Cornwall was to become the scene of action in unpredictable ways.

CHAPTER
TWENTY-NINE

DCI Drury and DC Boyns had returned to the hotel from their visit to the hospital in Potsdam wondering quite what to do next. The co-operation of the entire federal German police force was at their disposal, but what exactly did they want them to undertake?

"You know, John," said Mike Drury through a mouthful of very rich gateau oozing blackberry juice and cream, as they sat in the hotel tea room, "I keep coming back to your theory that Valtmeier will aim to head north to a Baltic or North Sea port once he has secured his body-part sample – if he secures one at all, that is. That may take him weeks; or maybe he already has a sample and is on his way. What are we to ask our German friends to watch out for?"

"Well, sir," responded Boyns, who had restricted himself to a small, plain biscuit with his peppermint tea, "I reckon we should focus on the transport, rather than on Valtmeier himself

– who of course will have changed his appearance and become unrecognisable.

"I had a good talk with that mortuary technician at St Josefs. Moving body parts around, for whatever purpose except disposal, needs a freezer. Frozen tissue needs to stay frozen – it's no good just keeping it chilled during the journey. Therefore, Valtmeier would need a refrigerated vehicle. Not just the sort of van used by mobile fishmongers or for butchers' delivery lorries, which chill to a low temperature but not to a deep freeze. His van would have to run a deep-freeze. In fact, I say 'van', but the generator unit and power required may mean that it is quite a large vehicle."

"And," interposed Drury, "presumably quite hard to come by, using illicit methods without a traceable document chain."

"Exactly so, sir," continued Boyns, "which means that Valtmeier might well be forced to use a conventional van-hire arrangement with a bona fide firm. And I imagine there may not be many of those in Potsdam, or even Berlin, with that kind of specialist fleet. I don't know, I'm only guessing.

"So, I suggest that this is our first line of inquiry with the German authorities. Then, sir," Boyns sought the attention of his superior, who seemed to have shifted his concentration momentarily to the gateau trolley, "we have to consider the next stage of the journey. If we're right and it's going to a port, the task for Valtmeier is actually a bit easier. A big trawler or deep-sea fishing vessel will have a capacious freezer anyway, these days. He only needs to find a skipper who accepts cash and no questions asked. That will be trickier from our point of view."

"Mmm, yrshlad, shee whashermean," replied the chief inspector through a blizzard of cake crumbs and dusted icing sugar.

Drury swallowed and found his paper napkin. He cleared his throat. "Right, John. I like it. So, we get our colleagues here to issue a request to all the relevant van-hire firms to alert them to every booking they make, till further notice. And, of course, to provide the records of any freezer-van hire in the past... what, ten days or so? Our Willi may have been quick off the mark."

He extracted himself from his comfortable chair and brushed the crumbs from his jacket. "I'll get on the phone now, lad. Have another biscuit."

*

Pietr Stetten had taken a taxi from Bristol Temple Meads station to a certain destination in the north-east quarter of the city; a small, nondescript warehouse not far from the vast structures of British Aerospace.

There he had met, for the first time, a colleague in the project who had set up the secret laboratory to handle and replicate the deadly virus that was contained in the sample dispatched by Willi Valtmeier onto the German fishing vessel. The two men had spoken frequently on the telephone in recent months, and the laboratory had been ready and waiting ever since the Ebola cadaver had been shipped from Spain all that time ago.

The arrival of the German boat at Avonmouth was expected in the next three or four days. Valtmeier had fully briefed Stetten on the identity of the boat and its filed passage plan, together with details of the Nipah virus sample from the patient's hospital records that his friend Meinhard had secured for him. There had been plenty of time for Stetten's chemist colleague in Bristol to adapt his systems in the laboratory to isolate and reproduce Nipah rather than Ebola.

All he needed now was the canister. Transport from Avonmouth to Bristol was not his concern – that was Stetten's responsibility. One last piece of the jigsaw puzzle.

Pietr Stetten was now on his way by local train to the docks at Avonmouth to meet up with the small-time crook he was paying handsomely to secure a freezer vehicle for the short distance from boat to laboratory. He had been assured that a suitable van was in this man's control and ready for any imminent arrival of the canister. But he had been in this game long enough to know that he could trust nobody. Money and threats were the sole currency in his world.

He had to see the evidence for himself. On arrival he would find a Travelodge or Premier Inn and take charge of the situation, even if it meant travelling back to Bristol in the freezer van itself.

*

The following morning, back in Potsdam, Mike Drury was having his substantial breakfast when he was interrupted by his colleague with a scrawled note of a phone conversation Boyns had just ended with a junior police officer at the local station. Two vehicle-hire firms, one in Potsdam and the other in Berlin, had responded promptly to their inquiries. Both had hired out a vehicle with deep-freeze facility in the past fortnight; the Mercedes-Benz from Potsdam only five days previously, to a single individual. It had been booked by a Herr Neumann, and was to be handed in at the firm's branch depot in the port of Bremerhaven two days later. It had been paid for in cash.

"That's our man." Drury nodded with resolution. "Or, if not, at least we can keep the reports coming in while we go up and investigate the possibility. Bullseye again, John, well done."

He resumed his cooked breakfast with renewed enthusiasm. "Run and pack, lad, and get a train timetable."

DC Boyns smiled to himself as he took the lift up to his room. With a bit of luck, on their return home to Bodmin, he might soon see his sergeant's stripes – not that he very often wore a uniform in his business. On a sergeant's salary, maybe he and Rosemary could afford to get married and set up a proper home together, at last.

They had been engaged for two years now. He knew she wanted children.

John Boyns felt a warm glow of satisfaction and anticipation as he packed his case. Surely he and the boss were now firmly on their way home?

CHAPTER
THIRTY

Jill and Petroc were certainly approaching home. The train pulled into the Penzance station terminus in the clear evening light. They debated whether to catch the number A17 bus to St Just, but with so much baggage agreed reluctantly that a taxi was unavoidable.

The stubby little ferry *Scillonian* had just made fast alongside its quay way over beyond the sprawling car park, its passengers disembarking and plodding down the greasy pier head, laden with their Scilly souvenirs, and probably feeling slightly queasy after a particularly choppy passage back, aboard what was notoriously known locally as 'the old Scilly Sick Bucket'.

As they stood in the taxi queue, the Tomlyns also watched a flurry of activity further out in Mount's Bay beyond the commercial dock. The harbour master's launch and a small tug were fussing around a large, anchored ocean-fishing vessel flying the federal German ensign and, Petroc noticed with interest as a

Coastwatch expert, displaying on its short forward mast the black ball-diamond-ball hoist indicating a vessel 'with limited ability to manoeuvre'.

I wonder what that's all about, Petroc thought to himself, but they had now reached the head of the queue and needed to concentrate on loading their bags into the boot of the taxi.

*

The two Cornish police officers arrived the following morning at the maritime federal police station on the commercial dock at Bremerhaven. The 'station' was little more than a concrete shed, but it housed two officers who knew the comings and goings of the fishing fleet and other regular shipping like the back of their hands.

The first point of inquiry was the van-hire depot at the dock. The local police had made some preliminary progress in advance of the officers' arrival, having questioned the depot manager closely as to the description and purpose of the suspect Neumann when he had returned the freezer vehicle.

Herr Neumann had been taciturn and had given nothing away as to his reason for the hire, but the manager had been surprised to see the interior of the van's insulated compartment still so pristine. The goods being transported must have been really quite small, and carried in a very clean container. Neumann himself had, as the respectable middle-aged manager put it, been typical of the brutish old East German type – shaven-headed, unshaven chin, wrap-around reflective sunglasses, open-fronted shirt in the worst taste; a former strongman now going slightly to seed. Average height.

Well, thought DC Boyns, *that could be Valtmeier, but equally it could be any other bloke. Not much to go on there.*

The next step would be rather more demanding: to find a connection between that particular vehicle and a boat of some kind. Who might have noticed the van and its driver close by one of the vessels in the docks? The port police agreed to circulate details of the Mercedes van and its registration number around the offices of commercial operators based at Bremerhaven. Drury and Boyns were not very optimistic that this would produce results – much more likely, in their view, would be that a casual bystander or crewman from another ship had happened to notice where the van had parked.

They were itching to deploy their detective skills on foot and slog around the docks themselves, asking encouraging questions, but neither of them had much German beyond '*guten Tag*' and '*auf wiedersehen*'. However, they were given port passes to walk at will, and decided to wander into the fishing-vessel docks to take a good look around.

The smells were overpowering. The combination of diesel fumes, raw fish and more raw fish was eye-watering. Mike Drury loathed fish unless deep-fried in batter, and complained bitterly.

"Blimey, I can't cope with this for too long," he groaned to his colleague. "I shall pass out." With that, his smooth-soled shoe slipped on a greasy patch of oil puddling the concrete hardstanding, and he fell heavily to the ground, ending up on his side with oil, water and fish scales saturating one leg of his suit trousers and the elbows of his jacket.

"Yikes, boss, no sooner said than done." Boyns risked a joke as he stretched out both arms and hauled Drury to his feet. But he could see that his superior had not registered what he had said, and was clearly shaken and in some pain. He looked around him and spotted a massive cast-iron bollard nearby, with a flattish top. He led Drury over to it and sat him down.

Drury rubbed his right elbow and grimaced. "Think I've grazed my leg," he muttered, and tentatively patted his thigh.

"We'd better get that seen to, boss," replied Boyns anxiously. "You don't want all that muck seeping through into a wound." He glanced back over the quayside towards the range of warehouses and processing sheds lining the fish dock.

At that moment, a young man wearing a heavy rubber apron and gloves ran across the standing from one of the doorways. As he drew near he spoke fast, with an inquiring uplift and a sympathetic expression, clearly offering assistance.

Boyns responded with a smile. "*Sprechen sie Englisch?*" he discovered somewhere from the depths of his dim recollection of GCSE German.

"Yes, yes, my friend," the fish processor replied, his face lighting with enthusiasm. "I worked in Liverpool for three years."

Boyns resisted the temptation to express doubt that Liverpudlian amounted to English. Now was not the moment. "That's good; thank you for coming to help. I think my colleague could do with some first aid and a clean-up."

"*Ja, ja*, we have a first-aid station back there where I work," the man replied, pointing towards the large steel building from which he had emerged. "Come, come, I will show the way."

Drury staggered to his feet and limped slowly behind the young German, with Boyns hovering solicitously. They entered the shed and were hit with a wall of fishiness that felt almost solid in texture. The temperature also plummeted down on them like a chill winter fog. Long rows of steel tables stretched the full length of the building, each laid with large plastic trays containing ice and fish being neatly sorted by species and size. White-coated officials methodically paced the rows with notebooks or dictating machines, recording, the British officers assumed, quality and likely market. Plastic slips with various reference numbers were planted in each tray on completion of their inspection.

All around them, processors in aprons and gloves unloaded, sorted and classified fish from stainless-steel trolleys that rumbled to and from the huge adjacent landing shed into which the catches from the vessels were deposited.

Their new young friend steered Drury and Boyns through all this busy, ordered activity to the far corner, where a door marked with a large green cross indicated the first-aid room. A man with a bandaged thumb emerged as they reached the room, and held the door as they went in.

Facing them from the far side and wiping her hands with antiseptic stood a huge and decidedly severe-looking matronly figure of classic Teutonic appearance; a bust before her like the Brisons, and grey-streaked hair held tight behind her head in a bun the size of a Big Mac. With her arms akimbo like a venerable oak tree, she stared sternly at the trio entering her domain, and lifted an eyebrow imperiously at the young man wilting beneath his heavy apron. "*Wass ist?*" she boomed at him, and then spotted the state of Drury's Moss Bros suit all down his right-hand side.

Instantly the imperial grandeur dissolved and Sister Siedler swept forward and gently lowered Mike Drury by the shoulders onto an upright plastic chair. She knelt and examined his trousers closely as her young colleague explained how he had seen this well-dressed stranger slip on oil and fall to the ground outside. She lightly patted her hand on the cloth and inspected her palm. "Hmm. *Das Blut*," she confirmed with a nod, and effortlessly raised Drury back up to a standing position, at the same time issuing instructions.

"Jacket and trousers off," his rescuer interpreted.

As Drury fumblingly obeyed, the contents of his inner jacket pocket cascaded onto the floor – wallet, pen, port pass, and Devon and Cornwall Constabulary warrant card.

The German lad bent to retrieve them, and could not fail to notice the last item. "Police?" he exclaimed. "British police?" He looked round at John Boyns, who nodded.

Sister Siedler fleetingly raised the other eyebrow before crossing the room to her cupboard for swabs, antiseptic and dressings. Then, as she carried out and completed her medical ministrations, DC Boyns explained to both locals the reason for his and his colleague's presence at the fish dock.

"With the help of your port police we are trying to identify which ocean-going fishing vessel took delivery of an item three days ago from a white Mercedes refrigeration vehicle with this registration number." He showed the fish processor a hire-firm advertisement displaying a colour photograph of the type of van, with the number plate he had written along the top. "The vehicle was driven by a male in his mid sixties." He gave the description of Neumann. "The vessel may still be here in port, or may have already left."

"May I, sir?" The young man held out his hand for the photograph. "If you like, I can take this to some of my colleagues out there and ask around."

Boyns glanced at Drury for permission and, at his nod, passed the paper over. "Thank you, that would be helpful. Please feel free to circulate the man's description as well."

The processor left the room.

THIRTY-ONE

Pietr Stetten paced the floor of the Port Authority harbour office back behind the soaring gantries of Avonmouth docks. Surely the *Essenstern* would have reached the port by now? Admittedly there had been a couple of days of rough weather with strong headwinds, but the past twenty-four hours had been calm enough. He had called in at the office three times now, and still there had been no registered inbound fishing vessel of that name or number.

Stetten kicked himself for failing to clarify with Valtmeier how he could establish contact with the skipper himself, while the boat was at sea. He was no sailor, and had only a hazy idea of maritime affairs – least of all the fact that mobile-phone reception was non-existent until a vessel was very close to shore.

He asked the port officer in the office at Avonmouth how to contact a vessel at sea in an emergency.

"If you're at sea yourself, sir," the official explained, "you would try on VHF Channel 16, which would involve an MCA relay if the vessel was not in your own sea area. German, you say? Well, sir, I doubt they would be listening on 16 until they were approaching the UK – but yes, it should be accessible in the English Channel."

"And if I am on land?" Stetten persisted, not understanding a word that the officer had said.

"From land, sir, ship-to-shore telephony; and of course you would need to know the number you are calling. You would need authorised access to that equipment, naturally."

Stetten wandered outside again and thought. Maybe, just maybe, Valtmeier had kept the *Essenstern* skipper's mobile number when he had finished fixing the deal. If, by any slim chance, the boat was sufficiently close to land reception – England or France – it had to be worth a try.

Valtmeier answered his mobile promptly. Yes, he had a phone number – for the mate of the *Essenstern*, Karl. "Boat not yet arrived, chief? Vell, if it's sunk, count me out. I've finished viz zis business. No more corpse hunting for me. I've done my bit. Best of luck, chief." And he hung up.

And that was the last that was ever heard of 'Willi Valtmeier', or, for that matter, 'Herr Neumann', both of whom vanished off the face of the earth. Their other personas lived on in a variety of guises and nefarious activities that are of no interest to readers of this story.

Stetten jabbed the numbers Willi had given him for the mate's phone, and held his breath. To his astonishment the connection was immediate and crystal clear.

They were where? The dock at Penzance in the county of Cornwall? What the blazes?

After an animated conversation in fluent German, the situation with the *Essenstern* became clear, and Stetten hung up. Instantly he phoned the van driver standing by in Avonmouth to say that there was a delay and that he must hold the vehicle ready at a moment's notice for the foreseeable future. Before the man could splutter too many objections, Stetten hung up again.

Back to Avonmouth railway station. Then change at Bristol and get the GWR train direct to Penzance. It was the last train of the day. He must be on it.

*

Home at last. In South Place, St Just, Petroc and Jill paid off the taxi and let themselves into the house.

"Well," sighed Petroc, "that was truly some adventure. What we desperately need now is a decent pot of tea. Pop the kettle on, love, will you, while I get the cases upstairs and sort things out? Don't trip over all that post on the doormat. Mostly circulars and adverts, I have no doubt – I'll clear them up in a minute."

Jill stood ruminatively at the stove, with a hand on the kettle. *That* was *an adventure?* she asked herself. *But somewhere out there is a conspiracy too horrific to contemplate, and which has not yet been resolved. I'm not sure I can relax back into the old routine until I know the danger is averted.* Thus she pondered while filling the teapot and plonking the tea cosy on top. Somehow she felt in her bones that the story was not yet over for her and Petroc.

And she was right.

*

The next day, Petroc wandered down to the Cape, to catch up on the news from his Coastwatch colleagues at the little station hut perched on the Cape's western edge. He was not actually on duty; not until the following week. He just wanted to get back to normal and resume his old routine.

His friend Geoff was on watch in the hut, and was bent over the powerful Leviathan binoculars fixed to the desk. "Oh, hello, boy," he said as he turned to greet his friend and colleague. "We've missed you. Good time in snowy Switzerland?"

"Interesting time, thanks, Geoff," was the reply; "in fact, rather more than we had bargained for. But that story can wait till we're up in The Welli. Anything exciting happened while we've been away?"

"Well," said Geoff, "pretty routine until yesterday, in fact. We've had an MCA alert that a trawler out of Newhaven shed its trawl and cable off Portland in that atrocious weather we've been having. We've been asked to keep a beady eye out – not that there's really much hope of spotting something like that floating half submerged around Land's End from up here. Still, I've been doing regular half-hour sweeps with the glasses. Not a sign so far."

*

In the meantime, what of our Cornish detectives?

Mike Drury pulled his trousers back on. The efficient nursing sister had finished off her work with a white bandage wound not too tightly around his thigh, and with strict instructions not to get it wet. No showering for a week, and he was to keep that leg clear of bathwater in the meantime. As for his bruised elbows, they would put themselves right in due course. All of this was in very broken English, but Drury was left in no doubt as to the instructions. After thanking the sister profusely, he and Boyns left the first-aid room in search of their young friend.

"And I must then find a gentlemen's outfitter, if there is such a thing in Bremerhaven," said Drury. "I can't go around in this ruined and stinking suit. I think I left my other trousers in Potsdam. I won't be allowed in anywhere."

"It is a bit whiffy," Boyns agreed. "Though from what I've seen of German tailoring, I doubt you will find anything quite as smart. They seem to go in for what might be described as unstructured bagginess. Still, go for the best, boss; it will all be down to essential expenses."

His boss looked at him doubtfully.

At that moment they spotted their young fish processor waving to them from the far end of the building. With him was one of the white-hatted supervisors clutching the hire company's advertisement.

"*Meinen Herren*, I think we have found what you are looking for," the young man called enthusiastically as they drew near. "This gentleman, one of my senior colleagues, has recognised the ice van and its driver."

Drury and Boyns shook hands with the supervisor, who apologised for having limited English.

"*Ja*, I see dis truck wit *der* man you descripted, three days back on Dock Number Dree. He were talking wit de *Kapitän* off ser sheep *Essenstern*, that iss wan off our regular vessels out off dis port. Zee *Essenstern* normally fishes in North Atlantic – not always, but I voud expect eet to haf headed vest into *der Armelkanal* – zer *Englische Kanal, ja*?"

"I am very much obliged to you, sir," responded Drury. "This is exactly what we were hoping to find. We will establish the whereabouts of the good ship *Essenstern* and pursue our inquiries."

The young fish processor translated, they all shook hands, and the British officers took their leave.

"Bingo," said Boyns as they made their way cautiously along the greasy hardstanding back to the port police station. "That was worth a leg injury, sir," he ventured.

Drury frowned at him. "Bloody well hurts, thanks very much."

The *Essenstern*, they discovered from the port office record, had left two days previously, logging her destination as the two-hundred-nautical-mile limit west of Ireland. She was booked for an eventual return to Bremerhaven.

"Stopping where on the way?" posed Boyns to his superior, who was limping along beside him.

"We'll find out when we get home, lad," replied Drury. "But first, I'm going to find a department store with a men's suits section, and preferably a cafe serving hot lunch."

CHAPTER
THIRTY-TWO

THE SKIPPER OF THE *ESSENSTERN*, HEINRICH KOLLE, and his mate and business partner Karl, were anxiously pacing the decks waiting for the three divers to reappear from beneath the hull, having inspected the tangle of plastic netting and steel cord around the starboard propeller and its exposed shaft bearing.

They had engaged a maritime engineer from Newlyn, Bob Hocking, who had taken two colleagues down with breathing gear, an acetylene cutter, and powerful torches. They seemed to have been underwater for an awfully long time.

Finally, they emerged and hauled themselves aboard up the fixed rungs over the topsides of the vessel.

"Well, it's not good news I'm afraid, skipper," reported Hocking. "We've cut through enough to see what's been going on down there. I can get the debris cleared and towed away for disposal, no problem. But unfortunately one prop blade has sheared off and the tight wrap of the cable around the shaft has forced the bearing at an angle out of its housing, with the result that the shaft has worn down about five millimetres diameter along a ten-mill section."

Kolle looked to his colleague for a translation. Having heard it, he wished he hadn't. "So," he muttered in German to Karl, "we don't go anywhere until we have a new prop, a new shaft and new bearings. We'll be here in Penzance for a week – and what about our insurance assessor? They may want to send one from home, unless there's an agency arrangement here in the UK. Thank God we were carrying no fish; just that canister. Well, too bad – that's not going to get to Avonmouth any time soon."

They were tough seamen, well used to crises and danger at sea. This was a nuisance and would have a cost in lost fishing time and sundry uninsured expenses, but they would cope.

Arrangements were made with Bob Hocking accordingly, the freezer kept running on its own generator, and in due course a berth found round the corner in Newlyn where the *Essenstern* was moored to await the necessary repairs.

Heinrich, Karl and their crewmates went ashore to enjoy themselves.

*

Pietr Stetten reached Penzance late at night. He found a taxi driver and asked him to take him around the decent hotels until he could find one that would accept an unannounced guest at that late hour. He was in luck – the first he tried was The Queens Hotel on the promenade, where he was welcomed courteously. He explained that he had travelled at very short notice in order to meet a vessel that had docked in Penzance earlier that day with mechanical trouble, and he was anxious to make contact with the captain as soon as possible the following morning. His host, the hotel owner, undertook to make inquiries before breakfast, but in the meantime hoped his guest would have a peaceful night.

Some hope. Stetten tossed and turned without sleeping a wink, despite the comfort of his luxury bed and the soporific sound of the waves slapping softly against the sea wall just outside his window.

So near, and yet so far. What if the precious canister of Nipah-contaminated body parts had defrosted when the boat broke down? What if it was discovered by Customs and Excise during the inevitable routine visit by a Customs officer on board a foreign arrival?

Stetten knew from Valtmeier that the captain and mate of the *Essenstern* were quite ignorant of the canister's contents. In exchange for the cash, they had asked no questions, and Valtmeier would not have answered if they had.

But the fact remained that the canister was not listed as cargo, nor declared to Customs, and so its discovery would be extremely awkward.

And what if it was confiscated, opened and poked about? The consequences did not bear contemplation.

Shortly after four o'clock in the morning he could bear it no longer. He got up and dressed, let himself out of the main hotel entrance, and wandered along the promenade. The dawn was just beginning to lighten the sky with pale green and blue away over the Lizard peninsula.

He needed a plan. There were two options. The first was to check that the cargo was still frozen and would remain undiscovered by Customs or police – in which case it could continue to Avonmouth in the fishing vessel as planned, provided that the delay for repairs was not excessive. Alternatively, if the cargo was intact he could himself hire a refrigerated van and drive it straight to Bristol from Penzance. The latter was undoubtedly preferable, and would probably be welcomed by the skipper of the *Essenstern*, as he could go off fishing and avoid the trip to Avonmouth altogether.

Stetten returned to the hotel for an early breakfast. His host had made the necessary inquiries of the harbour master. The *Essenstern* was berthed along the road in the dock at Newlyn. Stetten bolted his cooked breakfast, settled up and hailed a taxi to Newlyn, arriving at half past seven.

At the quayside against which the *Essenstern* was moored stood two police officers in uniform, a police car parked alongside with its blue light flashing, and a harassed Heinrich Kolle on the deck, gesticulating angrily at three uniformed Customs officials in high-vis yellow jackets.

Stetten turned on his heel, crossed to the seclusion of a nearby building in shadow, and leant against the wall, thinking rapidly.

*

DCI Drury and DC Boyns landed at Bristol airport after an uneventful flight. The bus took them promptly to Temple Meads station and they boarded the next train west, reaching Bodmin in the late afternoon.

They were exhausted; in Drury's case, both hungry and exhausted. The past couple of weeks had been some adventure and had turned out well, but the immediate task ahead remained urgent and high profile. Before leaving Bremerhaven they had arranged through its central police station a Europol alert for the *Essenstern*, as a result of which, of course, all the British county constabularies in the south and west of England had instigated port watches along the coast of the English Channel and Irish Sea.

An inspector at Penzance had taken the report from the harbour master, and had patiently bided his time to allow the *Essenstern* to dock in Newlyn before pouncing. Unfortunately, he had no idea what he was looking for on board the boat. The

Europol alert had instructed officers to intercept and hold the fishing vessel and its crew on suspicion of carrying undeclared and illicit cargo, pending further instructions. The inspector and his colleagues had therefore formally seized the vessel and cautioned the skipper, Kolle, and his chief mate. There had then been a language stalemate and an interpreter called for from Plymouth. The mate, Karl, had kept very quiet about his fluency in English.

Police, Customs officers and crew had then remained on board the *Essenstern*, awaiting clarification and the arrival of a senior officer.

THIRTY-THREE

N o sooner had Drury and Boyns slumped into their office chairs at Bodmin police station and stared glumly at the piles of paper, folders and Post-it notes cluttering their desks in an accumulated heap, than Drury's internal phone buzzed. It was the superintendent summoning him to his room.

"Welcome back, Mike," the super said. "Your German fishing boat, the *Essenstern*, has landed right on our doorstep. She's put in at Newlyn with some sort of engine trouble. We've seized her, and the skipper is none too happy. Better get down there and see if she's got what you're looking for."

Drury groaned. "No peace for the wicked, then. I'll take DC Boyns with me again – he's been doing a great job on this case."

"OK. And, Mike," added the superintendent sternly, "handle this very carefully. The Chief has the boys from MI5 and MI6 breathing down his neck on this one. If you find the material on board, it is vital that no one locally – Customs or police – is made aware of the highly dangerous nature of the stuff we suspect. And when I say, 'dangerous', I don't just mean health-wise – I mean politically.

"That said, if there's any risk of the container being damaged, or the slightest suspicion of leakage, get the boat cleared of all personnel, and the quayside, so we can get forensics there with all their protective kit on. I don't want the population of West Penwith dropping like flies from some deadly virus; not on my watch, thanks."

Mike Drury swallowed uncomfortably. "Quite understood, sir."

By half past six in the evening, he and Boyns would have reached Newlyn in a marked police car, and identified themselves to the constables at the foot of the ramp up onto the deck of the *Essenstern*.

*

Pietr Stetten had not been idle. From his vantage point on Newlyn dock, well back from the quayside mooring of the *Essenstern*, he had watched what was going on all day.

Not a lot. The police officers at the foot of the boarding ramp trod rather aimlessly to and fro all late afternoon and early evening. The Customs officials had departed, and the angry skipper had gone below with the police officer in charge, complaining and gesticulating in peremptory Germanic fashion. The deck and wheelhouse were deserted.

There was clearly an impasse. The frozen container could not yet have been seized, as otherwise Stetten would have seen its consequent removal from the boat and the crew being marched off to the police station under arrest. No police van or other official vehicle had appeared since he had arrived.

Stetten had a sudden inspiration. He remembered that he had the mobile number of the boat's mate, Karl, whom he had successfully contacted before leaving Avonmouth. What if Karl was free to move about the vessel unmonitored by the police on board? After all, even in port the boat would require a number of routine tasks to be undertaken. The mooring lines would need checking and possibly adjusting as the tide fell. The engines might need some consultation with the boat's mechanic, especially as something serious had clearly gone wrong to necessitate diversion into Newlyn in the first place. The motor serving the fish freezer hold was presumably still kept running and would need monitoring.

If only Stetten could phone Karl under some such opportune circumstances, out of hearing by the police, maybe something could be done.

He was desperate to get hold of the canister, one way or another. If only he had a refrigerated van standing by and could somehow get Karl to extract the object from its inconspicuous position in the fish hold. After all, it was only about twice the size of a large Thermos flask.

But of course, he had no refrigerated van. The more he pondered the circumstances, the more Stetten came to realise the consequences of the container's discovery and, being absent from the bill of lading and undeclared to Customs, its potential for disaster if and when it was opened for investigation.

He had no reason to believe that the authorities had any inkling at all of the contents of the hold. That they had turned up to question the skipper and prevent anyone from boarding or disembarking the boat may, as far as Stetten knew, be standard procedure for an unscheduled foreign vessel with no declared cargo of any kind. Perhaps they had already looked in the hold and seen nothing there. At any rate, the local police were clearly marking time for further instructions. It was now or never for Stetten to make a move.

He realised with despair that he no longer cared whether the contents of the canister were frozen or decomposing in the summer heat. At all costs they must be snatched from under the noses of the police and Customs. If not, they could trace the boat to local contacts in Bremerhaven, and if they then made a link, with the design of the canister, back to the hospital authorities in Potsdam, who knew what the risks would be to the project, and – more to the point – to Stetten's personal safety from either arrest or retribution from his powerful political masters?

*

At the same time that Pietr Stetten was reaching these conclusions from his inconspicuous corner overlooking the dock, Drury and Boyns were rounding the corner out of Crowlas on the A30 in a marked and powerful Volvo police car, the timeless vista of Mount's Bay and the fairy-tale castle of St Michael's Mount opening out before them in the evening sunshine. Beyond lay the town of Penzance, the fine tower of St Mary's church standing high above the slate roofs of the surrounding houses and old harbour wharf buildings. Around the curve of the shoreline would be their destination: the fish dock at Newlyn.

The holidaymakers, and the rush hour for local residents returning from their daily grind in Camborne, Truro or St Austell, had slowed the traffic to a crawl around the roundabouts past the out-of-town supermarkets and jumble of retail outlets littering the eastern outskirts of Penzance.

Mike Drury became impatient. "Time for the blues and twos, I think, John," he said, drumming his fingers on the dashboard. "We need to get on that boat."

With that, the flashing blue lamps on the roof and fenders burst into life and the two-tone siren split the air, startling the drivers immediately in front of them and prompting them to attempt all kinds of unlikely manoeuvres to pull over to the left to let the police car pass, their anxious faces betraying quite unjustified panic and guilt for some nameless motoring offence they may inadvertently have committed.

John Boyns pulled the car out into the oncoming lane and switched the headlights onto alternating mode. A clear third lane miraculously appeared as the traffic in both directions veered left, and, once on the dual carriageway, he put his foot down.

CHAPTER
THIRTY-FOUR

AT PRECISELY THE SAME MOMENT, STETTEN'S CHANCE arrived. A head of curly black hair suddenly appeared up in the wheelhouse of the *Essenstern*. It was not that of the skipper, whom he had seen gesticulating angrily to Customs officers earlier in the day, so maybe this was Karl, the mate.

Stetten pressed his mobile-phone key to recall the number he had used in Avonmouth.

He was in luck. He could see through the glass of the wheelhouse window an immediate reaction from the man inside, who lifted his own mobile to his ear. "*Ja?*"

"Stetten here. We spoke yesterday. Listen. I need that stainless-steel canister from your hold, and I need it now. If the police find it, you and your skipper are in dead trouble. You want rid of it, and I want it in my hands. I guarantee that more police are on their way, and they will know what they are looking for. Now's our chance."

A pause. "*Ja*, Herr Stetten, I follow you exactly. But where are you – how long before you can get here?"

"About ten seconds. I'm on the quay and I can see you speaking. How can we do this?"

"Well, *mein Herr*, the policeman here on board is sitting with the *Kapitän* in the saloon, waiting for his colleagues. There are two *polizei* at the boarding ramp. I think I can get the item from the hold, but I cannot just hand it to you on the quayside, can I? And you do realise that it is deep-frozen, do you not? It will defrost quickly in this weather."

"Never mind that," spluttered Stetten; "we're past worrying about preserving the contents. Let me think. I guess the canister would float? Just slip it casually over the side without too much of a splash, and I will work out how to retrieve it in my own good time. Your job finishes once the canister is in the water. But for God's sake be quick, my friend. Every second counts."

"*Jawohl, mein Herr*. Understood. The *Kapitän* will be very pleased and full of relief. *Danke sehr.*"

The phone went dead, and Stetten saw the head of Karl the mate disappear again below the windows of the wheelhouse. He stayed where he was and waited.

It seemed an age. Nothing happened. Then suddenly, onto the hardstanding of the dock, he saw out of the corner of his eye away to his left a large and powerful white car draw slowly and quietly to a halt some thirty yards from the *Essenstern*. Two men got out, both in dark suits.

Stetten immediately knew, beyond a shadow of doubt, that these were police officers, and that he had missed his chance. He was too late.

The policemen walked quickly up to the two constables at the foot of the *Essenstern*'s ramp and presented their ID. Stetten saw the larger of the new arrivals slip on the oily surface of the timber and make a grab for the rail.

"Steady, Chief, not again. That's a new suit," he heard his evidently junior colleague remark with a chuckle.

"Bloody fish docks," was the reply as both officers entered through the companionway doors and disappeared down below.

Stetten slumped back onto the old blue-plastic barrel in the dark corner between the two adjacent sheds where he had spent almost the entire day. He ached from head to foot, his feet in particular throbbing with heat and inaction. He had an intense thirst, and had eaten nothing since that early hotel breakfast. His temples throbbed with the beginnings of a migraine.

He supposed that he had better make himself scarce. Find a taxi back to Penzance station, and head back to London. But what then? He had abjectly failed, and would now in all likelihood be a hunted man. Another change of identity; another uprooting to some different country, trying to obliterate the footsteps he had left in the sand with his project masters, with the embassy, with his recent underworld contacts. He was getting too old for this game. Maybe he should think seriously about going home; back to the old, familiar life under a dictatorship that had changed very little for its citizens since the days of the Soviet Union.

He sighed deeply, and with hands on knees pushed himself up groggily to a standing position, from which he cast a final depressed glance over the quayside and the rainbow-coloured oil slicks floating in the dark water of the dock.

Also floating idly in the dock, reflecting the yellow light of the quayside lamps and bobbing gently against the submerged mooring rope of the *Essenstern*, was a large, shiny, cylindrical object, its top just standing proud of the surface.

Stetten froze, instantly alert. His aches vanished in a second. Just as quickly, his instincts restrained him from dashing out of the shadow to take a closer look.

The two police constables still stood by the ramp off the midships beam of the vessel, now in desultory conversation and gazing, unfocused, up across its bows. The steel canister had floated astern, and was well hidden from their view by the high transom and derrick of the boat.

Feverishly, Stetten looked about him for a long stick or pole of some sort that he could use to nudge the canister to within reach of the stone edge of the quay.

*

At the foot of the *Essenstern*'s companionway steps, DCI Drury called out. The local inspector put his head round the saloon doorway, eyed Drury's open warrant book, and beckoned him and Boyns inside.

Sitting glumly opposite was the German skipper, Heinrich Kolle. Conversation – indeed, any communication – had long since flagged as Heinrich had no English and the local officer no German. Kolle had naturally omitted to mention that his mate Karl had fluent English.

"We're still waiting for the interpreter, sir," the local man reported. "Meanwhile, nothing has left this vessel and nothing has arrived on it. The mate is on board dealing with various routine tasks, and the other crew were ashore when we boarded this morning.

"What exactly is it we are looking for, sir?"

Drury glanced at Kolle, and satisfied himself that he understood nothing of the conversation. "We have reason to believe," he answered carefully, "that this vessel is transporting a container of some sort, put aboard at Bremerhaven in Germany and destined for a British port – but not Penzance or Newlyn, as clearly this was an unscheduled visit on account of emergency repairs.

"The contents are likely to be hazardous, but I can say no more than that. They are also thought to require refrigeration and to remain deep-frozen. Our first task, therefore, is to examine the fish hold and any other deep-freeze facility on board. The container may not be very large."

"What a pleasant job, Chief," contributed Boyns; "rooting about in amongst a hold full of fish."

"Well, quite," Drury replied, "but I think we can rely on the local force for that job, eh, Inspector?"

"If you say so, sir," the local inspector acknowledged without enthusiasm. "At least they've been keeping the hold on freeze. Its generator has not stopped since they arrived. That's what you can hear under the floor."

The steady hum of a subsidiary engine had been constant. It was, however, suddenly interrupted by the clatter of footsteps overhead and down to the saloon.

One of the constables appeared at the door. "The interpreter from Plymouth, sir," he announced, and made room for a short, stocky man to pass.

"Good evening, gentlemen. How may I be of assistance?" he greeted them, presenting his ID and official authorisation.

Drury indicated to Boyns to take over from this point.

"This is Captain Kolle, the master of this vessel," Boyns explained. "Please inform him that we have seized his vessel as we need to search for an item that we have good reason to believe is illegal and hazardous. More particularly, we must inspect the refrigerated hold and any other deep-freeze aboard."

The interpreter duly translated the message.

Heinrich Kolle grimaced and sunk his head into his hands. Slowly he looked up, shrugged his shoulders, and gave every indication that he admitted defeat. With a sigh, he stood up and ushered the assembled company to join him as he led the way down to the internal access to the hold. There he unscrewed the wheel catches on the heavily insulated door, and flung it open.

A cloud of freezing and condensing air obliterated the doorway, then cleared. Kolle swept his arm into the space in a dramatic gesture and growled in German, "There. See for yourselves. The hold is completely empty. Nothing."

Indeed, they could all see that the space was vacant. No fish, but the corners and ceiling were still hazy with freezing fog.

"Too cold to enter without coat, hat and gloves," Kolle warned, and the interpreter interpreted.

Kolle slammed the door closed and spun the wheel catches. He stood facing the nonplussed group of policemen huddled in the passageway, and tried to look convincing. Fortunately, the haze of cold air in the hold had filled the corner in which the steel container lay, he had been relieved to see. Perhaps that might buy him time to think of something. Where was Karl, damn it? He hadn't seen him for an hour or two. How the hell were they going to get out of this? That confounded canister – frozen solid, but now definitely too hot to handle. *Still*, he thought to himself, *maybe I have satisfied these officers that there is nothing in the hold. Perhaps.*

Then Kolle's thought process was interrupted by a slow, mild enquiry from the young detective, Herr Boyns, standing before him with folded arms and a gentle smile on his face.

"Mr Kolle," he asked, "if there is nothing in the hold, why have you been constantly running the freezer generator motor all the way from Bremerhaven? Frightful expense, is it not?"

The interpreter translated. Kolle opened his mouth to reply, thought better of it, and closed it again.

THIRTY-FIVE

Pietr Stetten was cursing silently. He had found an old dinghy oar lying in the weeds along the base of one of the empty buildings near the spot where he had been lurking all day, and had crept around the corner with the intention of making a quick dash to the edge of the quay astern of the boat to try to reach the floating canister and bring it within arm's reach.

Unfortunately, he had chosen the precise moment at which the police interpreter had walked around the same corner from the opposite direction, and they had nearly collided with one another. With muttered apologies, Stetten backed off rapidly into the shadow, but not before the interpreter had looked him clearly in the face. The man would certainly be able to give anyone his description. *Damn and blast.* Mercifully the two constables had not seen the incident, and one of them had now accompanied the interpreter aboard the boat.

This, surely, was Stetten's best chance. The remaining

policeman by the ramp was evidently bored stiff, yawning and looking up into the sky for anything of interest.

Stetten crouched down as low as he could, holding the oar near the ground. He scuttled across the open space to the boat's transom, which cast an evening shadow onto the granite slabs. His luck held, for immediately astern of the boat was revealed a flight of stone steps down the face of the quay to water level. They were obviously never used as they were green with slime and seaweed. An ancient iron handrail, eaten away by salt corrosion, ran sporadically down the steps in vicious-looking broken sections with razor-sharp splits and ends. He grasped one of these and regretted it, but with a bloodied hand held on and slithered down two or three of the worn, slippery steps, coming to a sticky halt with one trousered leg submerged in the dock water and the other caught painfully beneath his own body weight, his shin and ankle severely grazed and raw from the rough granite treads.

However, he was now well below dockside level and entirely hidden from view by anybody standing on that quay, unless they were minded to peer over the edge behind the fishing boat, whose black-painted transom soared rather menacingly over Stetten's sore shoulder, its name and port proclaimed in huge white lettering: '*ESSENSTERN* BREMERHAVEN'.

Stetten paused for breath. He had dropped the oar while losing control of his descent down the steps, but it was floating docilely alongside the lowest tread, and he stretched down to reclaim it.

Now for the canister. Since he had first spotted it, and quietly blessed the boat's mate, Karl, the canister had bobbed in the breeze and tidal eddies along the length of the section of mooring warp that lay on the surface of the water. It was well out of reach of the oar.

He calculated that, with arm and oar outstretched, he could probably connect with it if he let himself down fully into the water and held on to the lowest section of rusty handrail with his other arm also outstretched. He tentatively lowered his suited form into the dock and was instantly up to his neck. Feverishly lashing around with his shod feet, he found a submerged ledge in the stone facing of the quay, and placed both feet on that. Leaning out as far as he could with one hand gripping the sharp end of the old handrail, he patted the water's surface with the blade of the oar, which dislodged the stainless-steel canister from the mooring rope. At the limit of his arm's muscular endurance, he worked up a slight movement in the water beyond the canister.

Slowly, agonisingly, the bright object gently floated nearer and nearer, and at last was in range of Stetten's hand. He abandoned the oar, grasped the canister, and hauled his weary, saturated body up out of the oily dock water, and sat on one of the slimy steps, aching and out of breath.

After a moment or two, he cautiously climbed the flight and slowly raised his head above the top of the wall. The police constable had now walked up the ramp onto the deck of the boat and was sitting on the bulwark with a clear view of anyone attempting to board or disembark. He would have to shift position to look aft.

Stetten made a run for it across the quay to the shelter of the nearest building, and froze, holding his breath.

Nothing. No shouts, no running footsteps. Relief. He had made it.

*

Meanwhile, Captain Kolle's optimism that the police had seen all they needed proved unfounded. DCI Drury had demanded coats, hats and gloves for himself and his colleague, and they both entered the freezer hold with a powerful torch provided by the local constable.

With the hold door left open, the freezing fog inside soon thinned out, and, with all the lights on, Drury and Boyns made a thorough inspection of the entire space, from ceiling to floor and corner to corner. One or two empty plastic fish boxes lay around, and a coil of polyester rope. Otherwise, nothing. They stood in the centre of the hold and paused, meeting one another's eye and frowning in disbelief. After all this time and effort – nothing.

Drury looked perplexed. "You know," he said to Boyns, "I could have sworn our friend Captain Kolle was looking guilty as hell just now, and scared stiff that his game was up. What have we missed?"

They searched again. Still nothing.

"A bit chilly in here, Chief," muttered Boyns. "Let's rejoin Kolle and keep up the suspense. That material came aboard at Bremerhaven – I'm convinced of it. Kolle thinks it's still here, but it isn't. Logical conclusion: unknown to him, someone's removed it. Another member of the crew? And, if so, it will have defrosted by now. Does that make it more or less dangerous?"

"Is it still aboard, or has it somehow been taken ashore?" contributed Drury.

"We've got to get our skates on, Chief."

Drury nodded, and they returned to the saloon. There sat the local inspector and constable, the interpreter, and an exceedingly glum Skipper Kolle, who looked up in resignation as Drury and Boyns entered.

"Please go and find the other crew member on board," Boyns instructed the constable, "and ask him to join us."

Boyns watched Karl's face very closely as he came into the saloon. Sure enough, he could not resist a brief expression and gesture of reassurance to his boss the moment Kolle looked up upon his entrance. Fleeting, but crystal clear. John Boyns missed nothing, and smiled to himself.

"Please would you come and sit at the table here with the skipper – oh, and perhaps you would shut the door first?" Boyns said rapidly in English to Karl.

Without hesitation, Karl obeyed, and then realised too late that he shouldn't have.

"So," continued Boyns, "fluent in English are we, Mr Mate?"

Karl said nothing, but it was abundantly clear to all that the barb had hit home. Kolle flashed him a startled and anxious glance.

"That will make our conversation so much easier, then." Mike Drury took over from his young colleague. "What have you done with the container of smuggled material that was in the freezer hold, Mr Karl? Not much good to anybody now, is it, all defrosted? If you've hidden it somewhere else on the ship, you'd better tell us now, otherwise we will have police forensics swarming all over the vessel for several days."

Karl cast a frightened look at Captain Kolle, but his boss had not understood a word. There was silence.

Then Karl put his elbows on the saloon table and dropped his head onto his arms. One could almost see the cogs of his brain ticking slowly around. He raised his head. "There is nothing aboard," he breathed quietly and slowly in clear English. "Nothing."

Another silence. Kolle squirmed uncomfortably in his seat. *What are they all saying? What have they discovered? Where's the wretched canister?*

"All right, then," resumed the chief inspector. "So what have you done with it? You do realise, I suppose, that the material in that container could kill thousands of people if it was released into the wrong hands – that, in fact, this is the very purpose for which you were commissioned to carry it?"

This time, Karl jerked upright and gripped the edges of the table, staring in obvious alarm at Drury. "*Mei... mein Herr,*" he stuttered, "please believe me, I... I have had no idea at all of the contents of any container in our cargo. As far as... as far as I am concerned we were booked to transport a frozen... well, frozen goods, but I had no knowledge of them... no, none at all, sir."

"And where," interposed DC Boyns, "were you bound with this particular cargo? Which port?"

Yet another long silence.

"We are bound for Avonmouth, sir, once we have our prop shaft and propeller replaced," Karl answered in a very small voice.

Captain Kolle recognised the word 'Avonmouth', and scowled at his mate.

"I see," continued Boyns, "but there's not much point in going there now, is there? Not without your cargo. So, what have you done with it? You've not been ashore. Chucked it in the dock? That could kill the entire population of West Cornwall if it leaked," he rather imaginatively mused.

Karl blanched, his face the colour of a soiled bed sheet, and his hands shook. "This man," he mumbled, "on the quay. He asked me. He was there and phoned me on his mobile phone. Same man who phoned me in Bremerhaven. He would pick it out of the water."

Here the police interpreter piped up. He had been feeling something of a spare part. "That might be the chap I nearly bumped into on the quay just now. I think I would recognise him. Medium height, dark, in a formal grey suit and tie."

Drury pointed to the door. "Constable, nip ashore and look around with your colleague."

The local constable dashed out and clumped up the steel steps onto the deck.

Boyns stood up and held out his hand to Karl. "Hand me your mobile phone, please." He thumbed the keys for the list of recent numbers, and pressed the 'redial' symbol on the most recent one. No connection. Hardly surprising, of course, to you and me, as Stetten's phone had been immersed in oily salt water for several minutes during his retrieval of the canister, and was now well and truly dead.

The local inspector was already on his phone to the Penzance police station giving the interpreter's full description of the man known to Karl as Stetten, and who was now presumably at large in Newlyn with a canister of deadly Nipah virus.

Kolle and Karl were placed under arrest and taken out to the police car.

CHAPTER
THIRTY-SIX

PIETR STETTEN HAD SHED HIS SODDEN JACKET AND transferred his wallet and cards to his equally soaking trousers. His socks he had wrung out and put back on. At the chandlery back on the Mousehole road he purchased a thick jersey and some cheap boat shoes. Once out of the shop and around the back he stripped off his shirt, substituted the jersey, and stuffed the shirt and tie into a nearby wheelie bin.

With the steel canister in the chandlery shopping bag, he began to trudge his way westwards up the steep hill towards Mousehole.

He had spent the night drenched and shivering in an abandoned shed, and, as soon as a nearby family grocer's shop had opened in the morning, had purchased some rolls and cheese. The grocer's wife had tut-tutted at his bedraggled appearance and had started to ask too many sympathetic questions, so he had made quick excuses and left.

And now... well... what now? Clearly, 'Pietr Stetten' had to vanish from under his project masters' control, and consequently from his existence as an embassy employee. For as long as he had cash, he could obtain a new identity and passport. That would be child's play. He had all the contacts, albeit in London and east of the Ural River.

But what about this canister? His immediate thought had been to ditch it somewhere; anywhere. Stick it in a bin, or throw it into a hedge. Then, on consideration, he felt that in some odd way he had a responsibility to keep hold of it. He alone knew what was inside it, and for all he knew the virus would remain active for some time to come, even though the body part was now defrosted.

Responsibility? Or was it in fact an act of self-defence; the possession of ammunition? For as long as he held this long, sinister tube, he felt powerful. In the last resort it might prove to be a means of evasion, negotiation, threat.

He gripped the plastic shopping bag tightly in his fist.

By the time he reached Mousehole, the sun had been warming the coastline for hours, and his trousers were dry. They were a sorry reflection of their pristine, hand-pressed condition in the embassy office, but were now a little more in keeping with the sea jersey and navy boat shoes. His unshaven chin had begun to lend verisimilitude to his overall appearance, and he attracted no attention when he called in at the baker's at the harbour and bought a Cornish pasty. This delicacy was a novelty to Stetten, and, all things considered, he thought he had never tasted anything so wonderful in his entire life.

His spirits rose, and he trudged up the hill behind the village into Paul. He had instinctively felt the need to get away from Newlyn without immediately retracing his steps to Penzance and the railway station, as that would be the obvious route monitored by the police, who he assumed would sooner or later be on his tail. The mate of the *Essenstern* had rid the boat of any incriminating evidence, but Stetten was in no doubt that the British police had somehow got wind of the nature of the illicit cargo before descending upon the boat the previous day. It was only a matter of time before Karl or his skipper cracked under police questioning and laid the trace to Stetten and the handover at Bremerhaven. And, Stetten recalled glumly, that official who had bumped into him before boarding the boat could well recognise him again.

However, by mid afternoon he was well west of Penzance, and it would be a long walk back to catch a train. He was far from accustomed to country hiking, and his new boat shoes were stiff and had rubbed his heels and ankles painfully raw. He sat down on a bench in a churchyard and eased off his shoes and socks.

Maybe the clever and counter-intuitive plan would be to go in the opposite direction to the railway station, and lose himself for a few days in the far west end of the Penwith peninsula, amongst the tourist crowd at Land's End, or in the nearby town of St Just which he had spotted on a map displayed on the harbour wall back in Mousehole.

The flimsy plastic shopping bag had ripped at the handles, and a split had appeared down the side. The steel canister was rather heavy. He wrapped it around as best he could and tucked it under his arm.

Shod once again, Pietr Stetten plodded off along the road to St Buryan.

*

Mike Drury exhaled loudly and slumped back in his chair at the Penzance police station where he and John Boyns had now set up an incident room. He had just come off the telephone to the chief constable after a somewhat demanding conversation.

The chief had not been at all amused to learn that an unidentified male was apparently wandering around West Penwith

with a container of decomposing human remains saturated with the Nipah virus. In view of the earlier scare over the body contaminated with Ebola that had washed up at Priest's Cove back in the spring, West Cornwall was becoming the focus of attention among certain central agencies concerned with State security; notably MI5. The chief would be notifying the Home Secretary that evening.

The man had to be found. He had certainly not boarded a train at any station west of the Tamar. The Torpoint ferry was being monitored, as was the Tamar road bridge at Saltash, but he could easily escape by car into Devon on the A30 beyond Launceston, or the Gunnislake bridge into Tavistock, or indeed via several other minor roads into North Devon. If he had a vehicle, the task was pretty hopeless.

DC Boyns was on the phone to the Hospital for Tropical Diseases in London, deep in conversation with a senior virologist about the lifespan of the Nipah virus in body parts now decomposing at ambient temperature. As he had feared, the advice was not encouraging. The virus could, depending on contamination density and other factors, remain infectious for a surprising length of time.

Boyns hung up and rejoined Drury at his desk. His news sank Drury into an even gloomier mood.

"Bloody hell, John. So what if we find this guy and approach him to make an arrest? He could point that damn canister at us like a loaded rifle. I doubt he has a firearm, so we will have to be mighty careful about deploying armed officers. Taser might be sufficient if we can get close enough.

"Get the locals to find a Taser-trained officer to join us. He or she must stick to us like a shadow. Oh, and get them to line up their best confrontation negotiator too. No, on second thoughts, get Jem Ladner down here from Truro. He can talk anybody down."

At that moment, a local constable in uniform entered the room to report. "A bit of promising info, sir. I checked with some of the Newlyn shops in case our suspect had bought food or suchlike, an' ol' Mrs Joyce in the grocer's down street says her sold some bread rolls to a feller 'oo was dripping with water all through his smart suit, early this mornin'. Also, Ben Lawry at chandler's on the Mousehole road sold a jersey an' sailing shoes to a feller shortly afterwards, who looked the worse for wear. Dark blue jersey, grey pinstripe trousers past their best, and new navy shoes. All sold 'im in one of Ben's plastic bags with his logo on. Not 'is trousers; he 'ad they on already."

"Right," Drury said, slapping his knees and standing up. "I want every inch of the roads to Penzance watched. He is bound to make for the railway station – or the bus station, which is in the same place anyway."

John Boyns frowned and looked thoughtful, but kept his counsel.

THIRTY-SEVEN

J ILL TOMLYN HAD BEEN STOCKING UP AT MORRISONS IN Penzance. After so long away, her trolley had been groaning with accumulated essentials and she had filled the car boot with at least five bulging bags. Several large items she had purchased for an elderly friend in St Buryan, and, after driving into town to pick up Petroc, who had been to the bank in Market Jew Street, they drove out along the A30 to Catchall and turned off towards the village; the great, tall church tower dominating the horizon. As they approached the outskirts, they pulled in to allow an enormous agricultural convoy of combine harvester, tractors and grain trailers to squeeze past in the opposite direction. Negotiating the grass verge alongside their stationary car in the narrow passing place was a very sorry-looking pedestrian, clearly hot and bothered and limping quite badly.

Petroc wound down the passenger window. "Can we offer you a lift?" he said. "You look as though you could do with a break. Where are you headed?"

The man raised his hand in acknowledgement but muttered that he was OK and did not have far to go. He glanced down at Petroc's face and a brief flash of recognition passed between them. The man then turned and resumed his trudge along the edge of the road.

The farm machinery having safely crept past, Jill let in the clutch and they carried on into St Buryan.

"You know," mused Petroc, "I'm sure I've seen that bloke somewhere before. I can't place him, but it was quite recently."

They arrived at the gateway of their friend's cottage, and Jill went in with the shopping. "Won't be a minute. Janet is bound to ask me to stay for a cup of tea, but I'll explain that you are waiting in the car."

Petroc gazed down the road past the war memorial and the church lychgate. The sun was warm on his face as he sat looking out of the open car window. After a while he dozed off. Janet Tregize was a lonely soul, and Petroc had resigned himself to a longish wait as Jill delivered the shopping and tried to extricate herself from her friend's rather desperate rush of conversation.

A good twenty minutes later, the car door opened and Jill settled into the driver's seat with a sigh. "Sorry about that. Poor old thing. Still, I now have the full detail of all that goes on in St Buryan."

She drove them slowly along the winding road around No Man's Land towards Crows-an-Wra. At the A30 turn-off to go up over Chapel Carn Brea, they again spotted the labouring pedestrian, in navy jersey and old pinstripe-suit trousers, resting on a lump of granite at the crossroads. He sat there with his head in his hands, his only accompaniment a chandlery shopping bag containing some bulky object on the grass at his feet.

"There's that chap again," exclaimed Petroc. "He said he didn't have far to go. Well, from here it's a mighty long way to anywhere. Maybe he just prefers his own company." He waved to the man as they passed, but he didn't notice.

The Tomlyns carried on over the hill, down and past Land's End airport, and before long had arrived back in St Just. Jill was just about to turn left into South Place when Petroc said, "Actually, can you carry on down to the square? We need some more booze from the Co-op. Hopefully there's a space to park. If not, just pull into Market Street. It's not a Thursday so the traffic warden won't be in town."

Fortunately there was an empty space in front of The Wellington. Petroc jumped out and slammed the door. Turning, he nearly collided with a couple of men who had just emerged from Warrens, one of whom had at that moment taken an enormous bite from the large steak pasty he had purchased there. His colleague was carrying a small paper bag with a modest cheese roll inside.

"Gosh, I do beg your pardon," Petroc cried, brushing from his jacket a quantity of flaky pastry bits that had landed on him in the near collision, and then staring in disbelief at the substantial person standing before him. "Good heavens! I don't believe it. Chief Inspector Drury? And Constable Boyns too. What on earth brings you to this neck of the woods?" Petroc shook hands with them both, and turned to beckon Jill to join them. "First Cape Cornwall, then Lausanne and now back in St Just. I have a feeling you must be tailing us," he joked. "Are we still your prime suspects?"

"Well, sir," replied Drury, "not exactly, but we are still on the same chase. I am very glad, in fact, that we have bumped into you and your good lady, Mr Tomlyn, because you may be able to help us."

"Goodness, are you still looking for more body parts, Chief Inspector?" Jill asked with some anxiety.

"In a word, ma'am, yes," Drury replied. "Could we perhaps talk somewhere in private? The matter has reached a point of some urgency."

"Come across to The Commercial, officers. We'll find a corner in there where we won't be overheard." Petroc led them over the road and into the hotel.

Mike Drury thought quickly. How much should he reveal? Was this very unprofessional? *No, the emergency demands it.*

He brought the Tomlyns up to date with the interception of the crew of the *Essenstern* and the sleight of hand by which the steel canister was now almost certainly in the hands of a man on the run in West Penwith; a man who in all likelihood was a central character in the international criminal project which Petroc himself had outlined as a possibility, back in the Hotel Mirador on the slopes of Mont Pèlerin in Switzerland.

"The male we are after is not one of your three jailers in that forest chalet. The two Cockneys are behind Swiss prison bars, and the German never went aboard the fishing vessel in Bremerhaven," DC Boyns explained. "We reckon that this fellow is one of the UK organisers who must have rushed down here when he heard that the boat with his crucial cargo had to divert to Penzance instead of continuing to its intended destination. He presumably came down by train a day or two ago, because he doesn't appear to have a car. If it's an international conspiracy, as you suggested, sir, he probably comes from London. Anyway, our local colleagues are actively searching for him as we speak. He is a male of sallow complexion, of medium height wearing a navy-blue sweater over dark tailored trousers and brand-new boat shoes, carrying a shopping bag which—"

"Hey!" Boyns was loudly interrupted by Petroc, who then looked around him suspiciously and lowered his voice to a murmur. "Gosh, sorry to butt in, but we have just passed that man over at Crows-an-Wra. He was about to walk up the lane over Chapel Carn Brea towards the airport."

"The *airport*?" Drury hissed in consternation. "Bloody hell – sorry, madam – is that his game?"

"I doubt it, Chief Inspector," said Jill calmly. "More likely he was on his way to town, here, where he can lie low for a bit in a B&B. He's not going to get very far from Land's End airport. Its regular service is the twenty-minute flight to the Scilly Isles, which would be a bit of a dead end. Either that, or he could fly round in circles on a scenic flight and come back to where he started."

Boyns was already on his phone to his local colleague at Penzance police station with the suspect's recent known location. "They'll soon pick him up," he said. "Well, Mr and Mrs Tomlyn, we are mighty glad we met up with you today. Saved us a lot of time. Thanks very much."

Petroc's mind was on something else. "Of course. The train! I thought I recognised the man. He was the chap – remember, Jill? – sitting opposite us on the train out of Paddington the other day. Very smartly dressed, he was then. Gloomy sort of fellow, clearly with something to worry about. It all fits."

"Paddington, eh?" Drury responded. "Good; a bit more to go on as to his operating base. Much obliged, sir. Now, if you will excuse us, we must skate back to Penzance ready to interview this fellow once he's been picked up."

With that, the two police officers departed.

"No peace for the wicked, my love," Petroc sighed to his wife. "We seem to be back in the thick of it."

CHAPTER
THIRTY-EIGHT

PIETR STETTEN WAS AT A LOW EBB, BUT WAS NOT stranded yet. He, too, had remembered faces. The pair who had offered him a lift were the same couple who'd been sitting opposite him on the train from Paddington as they returned from their holiday in Switzerland; a reference which had given him a flash of alarm at the time.

Pure coincidence, of course. Absurd to think otherwise. But what if...?

Stetten was not given to superstition. He was essentially a realist. But as he sat there on the stone outcrop by the roadside, it suddenly came to him that fate was not on his side.

He was not familiar with the geography of Britain. His only familiarity had been within the bounds of West London. Circumstance had brought him down this tedious peninsula to a small port called Penzance, and he was now trying to make for a little town to hide in, called St Just.

Suddenly, the realisation chilled him like an icicle down his spine. There was a connection between that wretched couple returning from Switzerland and this very place in which he now found himself. It was here, of course, that the Ebola-ridden carcass had drifted ashore back in the spring, thrown overboard in the Western Approaches by those damn Spaniards.

Full circle, then. This was where it had all started to go wrong. He had been thwarted by Cornishmen. Cape Cornwall – that was it; that was the rocky shore where that nosy coastguard had found the body bag. Right here.

A pity he had not instructed Coke and Jacko to do the fellow in, there and then.

Another icicle stabbed Stetten in the back. Of course, it was all coming back to him now. That inquisitive coastguard must have been the same Cornishman who had just offered him a lift; who had stared him in the face over a grubby railway-carriage table; and had been kidnapped on Stetten's instruction and incarcerated in a wooden chalet in the forest above Lac Léman.

Stetten calmed down a little. He knew who Tomlyn was, and would recognise him again. Tomlyn, however, had no idea who he was, even though he had seen him twice. What reason was there to suppose that Tomlyn or his wife associated him, Stetten, with anything remotely criminal or connected to their own recent adventures?

Stetten stood up, feeling very stiff. His blistered feet hurt. He started to plod slowly up the hill, wincing with each step.

A rough, grassy track led off to the left up towards the peak of the hill, and he decided to take it. The day was warm, and he needed to lie down somewhere soft and have a doze. He had not slept since leaving The Queens Hotel about thirty hours previously. He sat down on some heather and contemplated the view back towards St Buryan.

A car was coming up the road from Crows-an-Wra below him.

A police car.

It passed the turning to the track, and disappeared over the brow of the hill.

Stetten lay back in the heather and shut his eyes. The sun was hot on his face and he had no hat. Sleep evaded him.

His semi-comatose state was interrupted by yet another vehicle engine; this time coming from the other direction. He opened one eye and watched for it to appear.

A Land Rover. A police Land Rover. It roared past his vantage point and vanished from sight.

A lot of police activity for a quiet rural area, he thought to himself as he settled back down on the comfortable heather. *Who might they be after?* Instantly, he sat bolt upright. *Of course – they are looking for me! The captain and mate of the* Essenstern *have confessed. That official I nearly knocked over on the dockside will have given a description. I am a hunted animal. What the hell do I do now?*

Thoughts churned around in his head as he perched there in the heather of Chapel Carn Brea. He quickly realised that it would be madness now to enter the town and find a bed-and-breakfast. St Just might be heaving with police officers. Certainly Penzance railway station and all the local bus services would be watched. Somehow he must get food and shelter secretly, and sit it out for a week or so until the hue and cry died down and he could attempt an escape. By then he might have grown a beard.

At least he had plenty of money – at any rate, his bank account did, and he had a debit card. It would be some time before the authorities managed to identify him as Pietr Stetten, find his bank details, and trace his debit card use; if they managed it at all. His private administrative arrangements were deliberately complex. He had spent his whole adult life expertly covering his tracks.

No, the only risk now was face-to-face recognition and arrest in West Cornwall. He felt in his pockets. Four pounds and twenty pence.

He climbed to the top of the Carn and surveyed the land around. Away to the north-west, he knew, lay St Just. In the same direction, at the foot of the hill, he was surprised to see some kind of aerodrome or airport; clearly very small-scale and quiet. Best avoided.

He turned to the south-west and studied the array of houses and bungalows beyond Escalls. There must be a little food shop down there, surely.

He dropped down, crossed the busy A30, and dodged across fields and marsh around Trevorian to the back of Mayon, where to his relief he found a Costcutter. Stocking up on food and water, and purchasing a small, sturdy carrier bag, he followed a footpath down to Sennen Cove and ended up on the expanse of sand and dune that was Sennen beach.

He sat on a rock and unwrapped a rather unappetising tuna sandwich. In this, at least, he differed little from the scores of colourful holidaymakers likewise picnicking along the broad crescent of Whitesand Bay. For now, he was anonymous.

*

"I could do with some brisk exercise," said Jill on their return home. "All that sitting on trains and aeroplanes has made me flabby, not to mention that wonderful Swiss-French food."

"OK," agreed Petroc, "let's take the car to Nanquidno and walk the coast path to Land's End and back. One of my favourites. An hour-and-a-half should do it easily."

"Good idea."

And so, a short while later, Petroc and Jill set out along the path around Nanjulian and clambered up the rocky outcrop at Carn Aire before descending again on the perimeter path to Escalls, where they paused for breath and sat admiring the sweep of Whitesand Bay stretched out around them to north and south.

Black-wetsuited surfers rode the incoming breaking swell off Gwenver beach, sitting astride the longboards that Petroc, in his active youth, had known as 'Malibu'; quite an innovation in those days, and largely the preserve of the hippy dropout of the 1960s; the 'surfie' with his floral camper van and 'Ban the Bomb' stickers – those his father had tended to refer to as 'the ponytail brigade'. These days they were more likely to be chartered accountants or IT software designers.

At the far end of the bay, in Sennen Cove village, the modernist curved roof of the lifeboat station stood high above the surrounding cottages and seafront houses with well-justified majesty. Suddenly, the huge all-weather lifeboat itself emerged and slid gracefully down its greased slipway, entering the water with a great white bow wave and powering off west of the Tribbens rocks offshore in a wide circle before throttling back and settling its hull into the gentle swell to practise man-overboard rescue and what looked like recovery technique for injured crew.

Petroc adjusted his binoculars back to the shore and refocused on the bodyboarders and swimmers rather unnecessarily crammed together onto a very limited length of waterline between the red-and-yellow flags stuck somewhat arbitrarily in the sand by the young and beautiful lifeguards.

An elderly, grey-haired couple in old-fashioned bathing costumes resolutely and confidently swam out beyond the breakers with a firm breaststroke, some two hundred yards beyond the flagged limit, which they had evidently ignored with local disdain. Other beachgoers were walking the length of the strand; couples hand in hand, young parents with small children dashing in and out of the shallow surf, solitary walkers with rucksacks and hiking sticks.

Petroc's magnified scan of the scene was briefly diverted to a rather gorgeous redhead who was running across the sand to the water in a skimpy and alluring white bikini. This had not gone unnoticed by Jill, who slapped her husband's arm in mock disapproval. Petroc's binocular focus was jarred to one side, and picked up the form of a lone man walking slowly along the back of the beach at the foot of the fenced-off dunes that formed the backdrop to the bay.

Petroc lowered the glasses and stared, then raised them again, urgently adjusting the magnification to focus clearly on this new figure. "Jill." His voice was suddenly sharp and cold. "Take a look over there. That man with the shopping bags in the blue jersey." He handed her the glasses. "Do you see? That's our man."

Jill followed his pointing finger. "Hang on, I'll just focus a bit better... Gosh, you're right. That *is* him. What are we going to do?"

Petroc concentrated hard. "Pity neither of us brought our mobile phone. There won't be any police in Sennen. Why don't we just tail him until we can find some means of getting hold of the cops?"

They quickly diverted off the coast path up Escalls Cliff until they reached the quaint little bitumened wooden hut perched on the side of the hill looking down over the beach. There they hid in the shadow of the back wall with a good view back down to the path.

Sure enough, after a few minutes their quarry stumbled along below them. Once directly beneath, he paused and looked around him, seemingly searching for somewhere to go next.

Petroc and Jill froze. The man was studying the little holiday huts dotted up the side of Escalls Cliff. After a moment he appeared to make up his mind, and started to clamber up the slope – up towards the very structure behind which the Tomlyns were crouching.

THIRTY-NINE

PIETR STETTEN DESPERATELY NEEDED SOMEWHERE TO hide. He knew he could not wander along the coastline aimlessly till nightfall.

He clambered up from Sennen beach onto the coast path that ran along the base of the sand dunes, and headed north.

Up to his right, he spotted three isolated wooden buildings on the side of the hill, evidently former fishermen's sheds or some such, and now converted into primitive holiday boltholes. One or two looked habitable; served with overhead electricity wires and signs of domesticity. All appeared to be unoccupied at the present time; indeed, the nearer one seemed rather abandoned, with one broken windowpane and some rather grubby lace curtains flapping out through the hole in the glass. *That could be just what I need*, Stetten thought. *I could hole up in there for a week or two, nip into the nearby food shop from time to time, and play the waiting game.*

He turned off the path, and began to trudge up towards the little bitumened building, lugging his heavy grocery bag in one hand, and in the other the chandlery bag containing the decomposing body parts saturated with Nipah virus.

*

Drury and Boyns were both pacing the floor of the room they had been given in Penzance police station on Penalverne Drive.

They were becoming frustrated. The local police force had dispatched three marked cars and a Land Rover to comb the roads leading away from Crows-an-Wra in all directions, with a clear and detailed description of the suspect.

That was over four hours ago, and so far – nothing.

The assistant chief constable of Devon and Cornwall Constabulary had intervened, and had summoned a small police helicopter from Plymouth, which had yet to arrive. That might cover the ground more quickly and comprehensively, but Drury was sceptical that it could pick out an individual simply from a visual description.

Still, from a PR point of view, it might keep the Home Secretary a bit happier. Government representatives were getting very edgy. MI5 and MI6 were sending agents down to Penzance the following day. Drury hoped earnestly that he would have some positive news by then. But as yet, not a thing.

"Got any new ideas, John?" he asked his colleague hopefully. "You're the one with the brain.

"Oh, by the way, you know those exams you passed back along at Christmas? Well, as of now you are Detective Sergeant Boyns, continuing to be based at Bodmin. Congratulations, lad; you came highly recommended – by me.

"Now, to work. The crucial target is the steel canister rather than the man himself. At all costs that canister must be retrieved intact and unopened. The man we can deal with as a secondary issue. What do you reckon?"

"Well, sir, gosh," responded the new sergeant. "First of all, thank you; I appreciate the promotion and will do my very best to justify it.

"In my view, our suspect has gone to ground. He has made no attempt to catch a bus or train. If he has spotted our vehicles, he may have realised that he is their quarry, in which case he will now avoid the towns and try to find isolated shelter. He was seen coming up to Chapel Carn Brea, so may be looking for an old barn or shed in the Sennen or St Levan area.

"Take a look at this map, sir. I think we should concentrate our search, given our limited resources, on the ground south-west of a line across, like this, from Tregiffian Farm right down to Porthcurno. Forget the built-up areas of Sennen Churchtown and Cove, and Porthcurno itself."

"OK," his boss nodded, "but it's still a needle in a haystack. What about getting some local knowledge? Driving round in cars isn't going to do much. We need eyes on the ground. I wonder if our friends the Tomlyns might give us a hand? At least we wouldn't need to brief them on the background. Do we have their number?"

"If this was America," Boyns reflected, "we could have conscripted them as deputy sheriffs."

"Thank you, detective sergeant, but I think you watch too many westerns."

Boyns tried both the landline at South Place and Petroc's mobile number, which he had procured when they were in The Commercial Hotel in St Just. No reply to either. One rang in the house; the other buzzed in the empty car at Nanquidno.

"Well," Drury said, "keep trying, but in the meantime brief the MCA. We can at least get the coastguard people on the lookout. But do emphasise, John – no one is to approach our man or challenge him in any way. All we want is ID and location."

"I've an idea, sir. Mind if I borrow a car for half an hour? Just a hunch."

Drury nodded. "See you 'dreckly', then."

*

Sergeant Boyns drove fast along the A30, and pulled off right, down the steep hill to the car park behind Sennen beach. It was four o'clock, and he was just in time.

The RNLI lifeguards, in their distinctive red-and-yellow beachwear, were extracting their flagpoles from the sand, their little quad bike standing by to load them and a rescue board to put away in their lookout post for the night. There were three of them coming off duty: two tall young men and a more diminutive girl, all self-evidently as fit and as bronzed as mythical Greeks.

Boyns hailed them and they paused in their work. He presented his warrant card and addressed all three, explaining that he and the entire local police force were urgently searching for a rather uncomfortable, middle-aged, dark-haired man dressed as he described and carrying a heavy Newlyn chandlery shopping bag. He was dangerous and should not be approached. If they or their colleagues spotted such a man tomorrow, or before they left this evening, could they please telephone the police station number he gave them, and ask for Detective Sergeant Boyns? The lifeguards nodded solemnly and gave their assurance.

"Hang on," exclaimed the rather startlingly blonde girl, looking up at her colleagues in sudden recollection. "I think I've seen someone just like that this afternoon. Did you see him? I noticed because he looked a bit depressed, sitting on a rock over there eating a sandwich, and then mooching off along the beach dragging two large bags. He seemed to have trouble with his shoes, 'cause he took them off and walked barefoot up towards Escalls or Gwenver. Somehow he seemed out of place, you know – not exactly a holidaymaker."

Her two male colleagues shook their heads. They had noticed nothing.

Boyns was instantly on the alert. "What time was this, d'you reckon, miss?"

"Well, about half past one, I guess," she replied.

"I am very grateful to you, miss. Thank you. I'll follow up the lead." And Boyns walked fast back towards the car park, his phone to his ear as he briefed the chief inspector.

"We want officers on foot, sir," he stressed. "Can you ask the locals to form a pincer movement both from Trevedra Cliff behind Gwenver spreading south, and from Mayon Green behind Sennen beach heading north? We ought to have at least one Taser operator in each group, but I suggest no firearms. He's presumably on his own and hopefully well away from any other person. I'll start walking up the beach along the route our lifeguard friend saw him go two or three hours ago. I can meet up with our colleagues as they join me at Carn Barges."

Then John Boyns began to walk purposefully along the back of the beach, scanning the fenced-off dunes to his right. Before him in the distance rose the steep sides of Escalls Cliff, and the little cairn on its rocky outcrop way above.

CHAPTER
FORTY

A SHARP GUST OF WIND FLURRIED THE DRY SAND UP into coils and swirls in the late afternoon air. The wind had whipped round to the north-west. A dark grey cloud front, black in its underbelly, was fast approaching from over Cape Cornwall, the hitherto clear edge between land and sky rapidly obliterated by heavy squalls of dense rainfall.

By the time Pietr Stetten had reached the little privet hedge bordering the white-painted bay window of the wooden hut, hot and out of breath, he was feeling the dampness on his cheek. He crept around to the side of the building and tried the door. It was locked, but flimsy. Glancing about quickly, he satisfied himself that there was no one remotely within earshot, and put his shoulder to the matchboard.

It gave easily, and he stepped cautiously over the threshold. Inside all was dust and gloom, but the place seemed dry enough. Remnants of ancient wooden furniture stood forlornly around the single main room. Stetten found a small kitchen chair and wedged it under the handle of the closed entrance door to keep it shut, and to deter further entry.

A tiny and rudimentary kitchen was attached to the principal room in its own little low-ceilinged lean-to annex. A rusting and stained enamel sink, bereft of taps, and a chipped Formica counter above a painted wooden cupboard, appeared to be its only features. A small window, grey with sea salt and cobwebs, looked out to the rear, up the slope of the cliff.

Framed in that window, as Stetten gazed out of it through the gathering raindrops, a face stared unseeingly back at him, under the shade of a hand pressed against the externally opaque glass.

It was a face Stetten recognised. That confounded Cornishman, Tomlyn.

He retreated to the shadow of the interior and sat heavily on a rickety old dining chair. *There can be no doubt about it now*, he thought. Somehow, God knows how, those damn Tomlyns had been at his heels all along. This meant two things, he realised grimly. Firstly, they knew who he was and why he was a fugitive. Secondly, if they knew where he was, so might the police. So much for his hiding place, then.

He did some quick thinking. His gaze fell on the chandlery bag he had deposited on the floor by the door. He still had a powerful weapon. He sat up straight as another idea came to him. He had a weapon – and, potentially, a hostage.

*

Petroc and Jill had ducked down behind the hut as soon as they saw Stetten approach from the front, hoping against hope that he would not reconnoitre right round the perimeter of the building. The undergrowth close to the little extension annex where they were huddling gave a certain amount of cover, and they crouched behind it, holding their breath. They heard the thump of the side door being forced, and then silence.

"He is inside," whispered Jill. "What do we do next?"

At that moment the squall of rain hit them. They were without anoraks or raincoats, and were instantly drenched.

Petroc's curiosity outweighed his common sense. He rose slowly and peered into the grimy pane of glass in the back wall of the annex, shading his eyes from the heavy raindrops. The window was filthy, encrusted with dust and salt. It was impenetrable, and he could see nothing. He dropped down onto his knees again. "I'm kicking myself for not bringing my mobile," he muttered. "It would all have been so simple. Let's creep away up the hill till we meet someone with a phone, or knock on a door in Mayon Cliff and phone Mr Drury. He gave us his number."

They stood up, and the full force of the rain hit them.

"*Stand very still* and put your hands slowly on your heads. I am armed and will fire," a stern voice with a foreign accent declared from behind the bramble.

Petroc and Jill did what they were told, their hearts missing several beats.

"Now walk into the building and do not look round. I am following you."

They did so.

Pietr Stetten kept behind them with nothing in his hands but the stainless-steel cylinder, which he bore under his arm like an infantry mortar. Once inside, he closed the door and jammed it again with the chair. "Now then, my meddlesome friends, you and I need to have a long conversation. I imagine that you know what this large canister might contain. I will have no hesitation in throwing its contents over you or anyone else who obstructs me. Please do not waste time by pretending you do not know who I am. I know very well who you are. Things will go more easily for you if you co-operate, and answer all my questions. Now, do the police know I am here?"

The Tomlyns shook their heads, momentarily too shocked to find their voices.

After a weighty pause, Petroc cleared his throat nervously. "We just happened to spot you on the beach as we were out for a walk. The police are looking for you and have issued a description. We... we hid up here to watch which way you were going, that's all. Honest. Then you came up here yourself, so we were trapped."

Stetten looked at him in silence. Then, "Hand over your phones, please." He held out his hand.

Petroc stuttered, "We don't... we don't have them with us, otherwise..." and here his voice gained a little bravado, "otherwise the police would have been here by now."

Stetten sneered. "Well, my impetuous Mr Tomlyn, it's just as well for you that they are not here, then. You and your good wife would have been a useful human shield between the police and me – their bullets on one side and this deadly poison on the other, with you caught in the middle. Turn out your pockets, and that rucksack. I want to see if you are speaking the truth."

They did so.

"Hmm. OK," said Stetten, "we must now just wait here and see what happens. You could be here for a long time, so I suggest you make yourselves comfortable."

He pulled out of the Costcutter bag a packet of chocolate Bourbons, and began to munch them ostentatiously.

*

Mike Drury had been quick off the mark. His local colleague Inspector Harvey had pulled his response team off the winding roads and lanes, and all four had now converged on Trevedra and Mayon; eight officers in total, including two further colleagues equipped with Tasers. They spread out in two wide arcs, eyes sharp for any natural or man-made feature along the coastal slopes and ridges that might possibly serve as a shelter or camouflage for a fugitive.

If their target (whose name was still unknown) was still trudging northwards on one of the many paths, he would easily spot the uniformed figures slowly descending from way up to his right. There was no cover; not a single tree on this side of Land's End. Just acres of bracken, gorse and heather, low-lying and windswept. In that case he could be expected to panic, and the chief inspector's anxiety was that he would then run down onto the sand at Gwenver, armed with his deadly canister, and grab one of the many holidaymakers as a hostage. Drury winced as he visualised the possibility, or likelihood, that this would be a child.

With his binoculars he scanned the beach from his elevated position at Trevedra. All those happy families playing, sunbathing, bodysurfing, splashing about in the shoreline surf, quite oblivious to the drama playing out around them.

As he watched, he noticed a sudden flurry of activity on the beach; everyone migrating rapidly back to their little encampments of rucksacks, picnics, towels and windbreaks to haul out their anoraks or huddle under whatever shelter they could improvise. The intense squall of rain had, literally, blown onshore out of the blue, sweeping across from Aire Point like the theatre curtain across a stage; the obscured sun dimming like footlights, reducing the view to a grey murk.

The deluge hit Drury on the back of the neck like a blow. *Just what we don't need at this precise moment*, he thought bitterly. *Visibility down to about twenty yards, and binoculars useless.*

His search teams, however, were meticulous. Slowly but surely they investigated every collapsed Cornish hedge, every clump of dense euonymus bush, the dark shadow of every granite boulder.

The two teams from the south reached Escalls Cliff at about the same time; one working down from the residential spread of Mayon Cliff and the other up the slope from the beach and sand dunes. The dunes were tricky. Plenty of room to hide, down in the marram grass in the myriad folds and valleys of the lumpy terrain. But only for very brief evasive shelter. No one could possibly establish themselves there for any length of time.

No – much more promising were the little shacks dotted about above the dunes. These were well out of Mike Drury's line of sight around at Gwenver, but John Boyns gazed up at them from sea level, and, with two local constables, began to climb upwards.

FORTY-ONE

Pietr Stetten stood at the back of the room, leaning against the rear wall in shadow. He had a passable view of the hillside below, through the large but grubby panes of the bay window. Rain was sheeting against the glass, and his vision was limited to about fifty yards. The sea itself was quite obscured, merging into the murk of the dark sky. Out of that murk appeared three figures in a straggling line, slowly climbing the slope. Police officers.

The Tomlyns sat together on the floor, ruminating on their propensity for getting kidnapped.

"This is becoming a habit," Petroc murmured to his wife gloomily.

"Be quiet, you," snarled Stetten. He crossed the room and reinforced the wedged entrance door with a baulk of timber that had been a shelf. "If you two make the slightest sound I assure you that you will bitterly regret it," he hissed, and then squatted down himself behind a table in the centre of the room. The Tomlyns were under the table, an old pair of matching chairs effectively screening all three of them from the bay window.

A few minutes later a loud thump on the door jolted all three occupants, Petroc bumping his head against the underside of the table. Stetten glared at him and brandished the steel canister, making as if to release the spring clips on its lid. Petroc smothered a groan.

All three of them watched the door. The handle was being turned, both ways repeatedly. Another thump, as of a shoulder put to the door. But the chair and shelf wedges held. The light, such as it was, suddenly diminished against the bay window. Stetten could just determine three heads, three faces, obscuring the panes and disappearing again. Seconds later, they all heard scratching and thumping on the little kitchen window at the rear of the hut. Some low, murmuring voices. Then silence.

The silence held. Stetten crept across the floor on his hands and knees and slowly raised his head above the windowsill. The three police officers were walking away around the contour of the hill towards another little hut perched slightly higher to the south.

Stetten breathed a sigh of relief. "Well, that is excellent, my friends. The police have come and gone. We can just settle down here, nice and cosy. Here, have something to eat." He threw down at Jill's knees the remains of the packet of biscuits.

Jill reached out for it, and happened to glance through the internal doorway at the small window of the kitchen beyond. From behind the glass was a face squinting into the room: a man wearing a black peaked baseball cap with 'POLICE' written in white capitals across the brow.

"As the police have gone away," she whispered after a moment's frantic thought, "could we stretch our legs and walk about a bit? I'm getting cramp."

Stetten looked out again. The three officers were a long way off now. He nodded and stood up, backing into a corner and clasping the canister to his chest. "No funny business, now. And no noise."

Jill and Petroc struggled to their feet and shook out their arms and shoulders in relief.

Jill quietly moved back a few steps into the doorway between the principal room and the rear kitchen. Slowly and nonchalantly she edged further back and leant against the old sink beneath the kitchen window. She was still in full view of Stetten, but awaited her chance. Then Petroc raised his arms behind his neck and stretched, briefly obstructing that view. Jill reached back with one arm and with her forefinger wrote in quivery letters, 'SOS', in reverse, through the grime of the window glass. She did not look round.

Petroc wandered away to one side, and Jill remained calmly with her back to the kitchen sink, her figure blocking the window. She closed her eyes, and hoped.

After what seemed like an age, as she turned her head slightly to one side, she sensed rather than saw the light from the little window behind her briefly diminish and reappear. Someone had once again put their face to the glass to peer inside. Jill prayed it was the same policeman. Surely he would now have noticed something different in the windowpane: a plea for help that had not been there moments before?

*

DS Boyns and his two colleagues had reached the third hut, having drawn a blank at the first one with the white bay window, and another further up. This one was occupied – not by their fugitive, but by an elderly, bearded man in a smock, around whom there hung an all-pervading aroma of turpentine and oil paint. The entire space was taken up with stacks of stretched canvases, framed and unframed, and a huge easel upon which stood an unfinished and rather flamboyant portrait of a young woman, the actual specimen of whom lay draped across an ancient chaise longue in the corner of the studio, entirely and unselfconsciously naked.

Boyns made his excuses and a hasty retreat. He looked up the hill to Mayon Cliff. His other southern team of officers had made its way down the slope, and had just reached the back of the bitumened hut that he and his colleagues had left ten minutes before. There were no more shacks to investigate, and so Boyns and his men started to retrace their steps to join the team they had spotted. They could then compare notes and resume their search northwards around the coastline.

As they trudged across to join their colleagues, the sun reappeared from behind the curtain of black cloud which had moved on over Land's End. The warmth flowed over the hillside, and the figures down on the beach began to emerge from the improvised shelters under which they had been cowering. Children raced out again across the sand with their beach balls and bellyboards, their parents and grandparents busying themselves mopping up the drenched picnic baskets and towels. Sheets of brightly coloured sopping beachwear began to be spread out over the smooth white boulders at the back of the beach to dry off in the gaining sunlight.

DCI Drury and his team had now clambered around from the base of Escalls Cliff, and, as visibility improved, could see Boyns and the other officers closing on a third group of police who appeared to be concentrated at the rear of a black-bitumened summer house on the hillside above. Something in their manner alerted Drury to the possibility that they had seen or heard activity in the little building that warranted careful investigation.

I hope to goodness our man is in there, he thought gloomily. *My pincer movement has now come full circle, with absolutely no luck so far.*

As he and his men were still down on the coast path, Drury's TETRA suddenly buzzed. "Sergeant Hicks here, sir. We are up behind the black shack with a white-painted bay window you can see from your position. Please can you and your team get back out of sight of that window? There's something odd going on here. Someone inside has just this minute written 'SOS' with their finger in the muck on the rear window. It wasn't there a few minutes ago. If our target suspect is in this shack, it looks as though someone else is there as well, and none too happy about it.

"Sergeant Boyns will be with us any minute from across the way, and I've alerted him to keep well clear of the line of sight from the front window. Shall we force an entry, or call a warning from outside first, sir?"

"OK, Sergeant. Understood. Await Sergeant Boyns and follow his instructions. He has my authority to proceed at his discretion."

CHAPTER
FORTY-TWO

JILL WAS THINKING VERY RAPIDLY, ACUTELY AWARE that she alone had any inkling of what was going on beyond the thin wooden wall of the shack.

If the police outside had realised the implication of the 'SOS' message, they would now know that, if the man they were chasing was inside, he had a hostage. At least that would mean that they would not burst in with guns blazing (she acknowledged that she was an addict of those Nordic crime series on the television), but would presumably try some other technique to surprise, or maybe persuade him.

But then what? She and Petroc were not just any old hostages. They were the very individuals who had the information and recognition as witnesses to the entire criminal set-up. Their identification of the offenders, their names and connections could put them all away for a great many years – indeed, they were crucial to the success of a Crown Court prosecution.

Their kidnapper knew this all too clearly. He would have no means of escape now, once the police had banged on the door. His sole bargaining chip was the steel canister of Nipah-infested putrefying flesh that he held clasped to his chest. All he had to do on hearing the knock on the door or the breaking of window glass was to unclip the lid, grab Jill or her husband by the neck and threaten loudly to pour the contents all over their face, perhaps for good measure grazing or cutting their cheek to create a direct blood contamination.

These lurid images flashed before Jill's eyes in a matter of seconds. *It's up to me to do something*, she thought, *and I've got to do it quickly. I must create a diversion somehow. I need to distract his attention just at the right moment.*

Still leaning as nonchalantly as possible against the edge of the kitchen sink, she casually looked around the little room that had clearly been tacked onto the original square shack. High up on the wall of the kitchen facing her, to one side of the internal doorway, she noticed in the shadowy murk a wooden shelf. On the shelf, wreathed in cobwebs, was a row of ancient, rusted steel saucepans. The shelf looked none too secure, both wall brackets coming away from the timber wall, their screws presumably corroding in the salt-laden atmosphere.

Jill tensed, ready to move at a moment's notice.

*

DS Boyns and his team had now reached the back of the hut and joined their colleagues crouched behind the euonymus bushes surrounding the old patch of overgrown garden. He quietly consulted his fellow sergeant as to tactics.

"If he's got the lethal material we think he's got," he whispered, "then I reckon we use the element of surprise. A hailed warning could put any hostage more at risk of restraint and injury. What do you think?"

His colleague thought for a moment and nodded.

"Right, lads," Boyns said. "I want you, Constable, to crawl to the back window and, when I give the signal, reach up and tap the glass three times. That may alert whoever wrote the 'SOS', but hopefully not our target.

"Immediately, then, my team will rush the side door, Taser officer at the front with me. Sergeant Hicks and his team will position themselves around the exterior of the building, with a close eye on the bay window in case he makes a leap for that. All clear? Any questions? No? OK, then. Let's go."

Moments later, just as a particularly large and powerful police officer stuck a hefty Size 14 boot into the flimsy entrance door, a terrific crash of metal objects landing on a concrete floor rang out from the rear of the shack. Ancient, weighty Aga saucepans clashed and bounced, followed by the sound of breaking glass as Constable Angwin put his elbow through the little rear window, reached in to open the casement, and neatly launched himself through the opening, landing on the floor alongside Jill and amongst the assorted scattered cookware.

"By 'eck – Jill, my luvver! What the 'ell are you doin' 'ere?" he just had time to say to his next-door neighbour in St Just, before standing to his full height and girth, blocking the internal doorway.

As the saucepans cascaded to the floor, Pietr Stetten whipped round and stared into the kitchen. One eye caught a black-sleeved elbow barging through the glass of the rear window; the other instantaneously glanced at the old kitchen chair lodged under the handle of the entrance door, disintegrating like so much dry kindling as the impact of a police boot slammed the matchwood door wide open and sent the puny shelf buttress spinning across the worn linoleum.

Swivel-eyed, Stetten clasped the canister tighter to his chest and backed to the far side of the table, behind which Petroc

Tomlyn had instinctively crouched. Stetten grabbed his shoulder like a vice.

"One move and you're a dead man," he snarled, whipping the clips off the lid of the steel canister.

One policeman now loomed in the kitchen doorway. Two others stood in the entrance; a Taser in the hands of the officer in uniform. Several more officers stood outside, looking in.

"Police," announced the officer in civvies, rather unnecessarily. "Please put that container down on the table, gently and calmly now. We wish to talk to you. Put your hands in the air and move slowly away from that gentleman, around to the side of the table. Do it now, please."

Stetten moved not a muscle. With a strained rictus smile on his face, he proceeded unhurriedly to open the canister above Petroc's head, and tip it at an angle while unfastening the remaining clips.

John Boyns noticed his colleague raising his yellow Taser, but steadily eased his arm across and lowered the device.

"Very wise, Mr Policeman," Stetten jeered in a cracked voice. "One false move and your little spy gets a face full of Nipah virus. Very, very nasty. Once it's in his eyes, ears or mouth he's as good as dead.

"Now, a little negotiation, if you please. I keep hold of Tomlyn and the canister; you all back off one hundred metres, and then I—"

But Stetten spoke no further. In the kitchen, behind the bulk of Constable Angwin, the last remaining Aga pan toppled off the remnants of the high shelf and crashed like an orchestral cymbal into the jumble of steel pots littering the concrete floor.

Everybody jumped involuntarily – except Constable Angwin, who was made of sterner stuff. Petroc's shoulder jolted against Stetten's knee. Stetten's arm, holding the canister, jerked forward. His movement tilted the canister, and the unclasped lid dropped off into Petroc's lap.

Stetten made a hasty attempt to right the container, but it was too late. Petroc had unthinkingly raised his face up to the doorway on hearing the crash, and received, right on the nose, the entire contents of the dreaded canister held above his head.

FORTY-THREE

TRUST AMONG CROOKS IS AN INTERESTING phenomenon. It is often very deep and long-lasting. The concept of brotherhood, family or clan loyalty; of history and tradition in certain localities always to support your colleagues in crime; this is habitually genuine and willing. Other forms of trust in criminal circles are a great deal less altruistic, relying for their efficacy on fear, gangland 'honour', recompense or retribution.

In Pietr Stetten's case, he had placed his trust in the category of recompense, and indeed had paid handsomely for the services of his hirelings in the project for which he had been commissioned, and which had now reached its momentous denouement in a little summer-house shack perched on the coastline of West Cornwall. He had expected loyalty and honour from those whom he had enriched.

*

Petroc opened his eyes. His nose hurt a little, from the surprisingly lumpy dead weight of three objects hitting it in quick succession. Funny, though – no smell. He had fleetingly expected his nostrils to be assaulted with the most revolting stench of rancid, fetid, decaying human flesh.

The objects had left no residue on his face, and had dropped to the floor. He looked about him on the dusty lino and studied the nearest one with some bafflement. Tentatively, he stretched out a hand and picked it up. Suspended from his fingers was a long brown woollen sock, clearly filled to the brim with builders' grey sand, now overflowing into his lap.

Petroc looked up at Stetten and met his appalled gaze. Not quite knowing what else to do, he lifted the stuffed sock up for all to see, and handed it to Stetten almost apologetically. In a daze, Stetten took it. Petroc retrieved the other two similarly stuffed socks (one of which was blue), and hoisted them carefully up onto the table.

Nobody had spoken since the saucepan had fallen. Somehow, time had become suspended.

The trance was suddenly broken by Pietr Stetten, who collapsed onto a dining chair and buried his head in his hands. "That bloody Valtmeier!" They all heard his muffled tone of despair.

"You've done for me, Valtmeier, you unspeakable bastard."

With that, he was quietly led away in handcuffs by Constable Angwin.

CHAPTER
FORTY-FOUR

THE END OF THE SUMMER WAS IN THE AIR. THE STILL-warm sunshine that seemed to increase in intensity during the course of the afternoons was now suddenly giving way to a sharp drop in temperature in the shade. The welcome cooling breezes on the corners of Bank Square in St Just now whipped a chill gust around the edges of the grey buildings.

After sunset the jerseys and sweaters appeared; even one or two scarves. The faded maroon double doors of the great 'Miners' Chapel', looming its bulk at the far end of Chapel Street, somehow betokened the dulling of summer heat by the imminent cool of autumn and early winter. The grass in the chapel yard lay down, dank and browning at the tips. Even the inky blackberries on the hedgerow brambles were losing their succulence and beginning to shrivel.

The edge of the Atlantic Ocean at the far end of the Cot Valley, picture-postcard blue in the warmth of recent months, grumbled now over the loose, round boulders in battleship grey, the cheerful snow-white breakers beloved of the holiday surfers transfigured into hollow, leaden tunnels of roaring menace. Around the corner of Carn Gloose to the north, Cape Cornwall projected, undaunted, out into the sea in defiance of the elements; its iconic smokestack (rather incongruously restored through the charitable funds of a famous purveyor of baked beans) standing proudly at its peak.

On the western face of the Cape, braced bravely on its rock plateau, buffeted by the strong south-westerly ('Five or Six, increasing Force Seven; rain later') stood the little white-painted Coastwatch station.

Petroc Tomlyn leant into the wind as he rounded the corner of the path and slogged up the steps alongside the dressed-granite retaining wall, salt spray clouding the lenses of his glasses and forming miniature bauble decorations all over the front of his woollen uniform jersey. He hauled himself up the steep flight and opened the door of the station hut, mindful from long experience not to let it fling back off its hinges in the relentless wind.

"Afternoon, Geoff," Petroc greeted his colleague cheerfully. "Lovely day for it. Anything interesting on your watch? It's looking a bit lively out there."

"Not a thing, Petroc, boy. I'll leave you to it. I've got to be off up Camborne dreckly, so I'd better be making my way.

"Oh – one thing, though. Here, take a look through my binoculars. Down there on that rock, just off the base of the old mine stamps – can you see that dark sheet there, wedged in the gap? Some sort of canvas tarp or bag by the looks of 'im. What d'you reckon it might be, then?"

Petroc slowly focused the binoculars in the direction in which his colleague was pointing. He looked steadily at the grey, sodden material screwed up on the black-granite outcrop far below. He lowered the glasses and paused.

"I really don't know, Geoff, and to be perfectly frank, I don't much care."

ACKNOWLEDGEMENTS

THE INTERNATIONAL CRIME THEME UNDERLYING THIS story was conceived long before the 2018 Novichok scandal in Salisbury, and well before the Covid-19 pandemic with its alarmingly swift global proliferation in 2020. The combined features of these two crises in the scenario of a novel may appear insensitive, and I ask the indulgence of any reader who may have been affected by either of those calamities.

My thanks to Lalla Hitchings once again for her skill in deciphering and typing my Biro manuscript largely written aboard a small sailing cruiser in wet weather.

Thanks especially to the engaging and friendly team at The Book Guild in accepting this offering for publication, and for Rosie Lowe's prompt and enthusiastic response to all my queries. I must particularly credit my copy editor Faye Booth for her meticulous attention to detail, and for her pointing out several anachronisms from the pen of an almost-seventy year old in the dialogue of characters less than half my age.

Also to my wife Biddy, for a family history interest of her own which prompted a delightful trip to the shores of Lac Leman in Switzerland. I acknowledge too her oft-repeated reminder that I am only half Cornish, the other half being North Devonian.

Nonetheless, my main tribute is reserved to my paternal Cornish forebears who have instilled in me a lifelong love for one tiny corner of West Cornwall, where my family has had an unbroken presence for at least 300 years and which continues to this day.

Richard Trahair